Out of My
SHELL

Out of My SHELL

JENNY GOEBEL

Scholastic Press | New York

Library of Congress Cataloging-in-Publication Data available

ISBN 978-1-338-25955-1

10 9 8 7 6 5 4 3 2 1   19 20 21 22 23

Printed in the U.S.A. at Berryville Graphics in Berryville, Virginia   37

First edition, July 2019

Book design by Abby Dening

With immense love, this book is dedicated to the Davenport Family,

James, Kristen, Madison, Macy, Lydia, and Noah.

**Sea turtles are reptiles and must rise to
the surface to breathe. However, a sea turtle
can hold its breath and remain underwater
for several hours at a time.**

My little sister, Lanie, was hogging the armrests. She was in the middle seat, between Mom and me. Lifting herself with her hands, she tucked her knees to her chest and swung back and forth in the small space between rows. She was practically performing gymnastics on the airplane. She was excited for our trip—genuinely and wholeheartedly excited. As badly as I wanted to be, too, I couldn't bring myself to feel even a shimmer of anticipation.

When the flight attendant took my drink order a few minutes later, I could hear myself saying, "apple juice," and "thank you." But what I was thinking was, *You've got to keep it together, Liv.*

Our family was minus one, and even though Lanie was

oblivious—bouncing in her seat and bursting with giggles—I was on the verge of falling apart. I couldn't stop glancing at the open seat across the aisle. The place where Dad should've been sitting.

Mom was in rough shape, too. Her fingers drummed the armrest almost the entire flight. She got even more frazzled after the plane landed in Tampa and she had to rent a car. Her legs moved restlessly as she stood in line, creating little ripples in her long, flowery skirt. I wished I could help, but I also knew the rental car company would never turn keys over to me.

Dad had always been the one to step up to the counter. Mom usually corralled our luggage and squeezed droplets of hand sanitizer into Lanie's and my hands, even though we'd already washed them in the airport bathroom.

This time, Mom skipped the hand sanitizer and shot me a pleading look as the woman behind the counter took her credit card. I followed Mom's line of sight to where my sister was standing, hovering really, over a stranger's wheeled bag. Lanie gave the luggage a slight shove, testing its unrestricted movement.

"Lanie," I cautioned, and lunged for her arm. I wasn't quick enough. My fingers snatched empty air as she belly flopped onto the bag. "Wheeeee," she cried, rolling past the Enterprise Rent-A-Car sign and bowling right into a group of tourists.

There were a few yelps, some groans. Two pairs of sunglasses and a beach hat went flying.

Thankfully, Mom was too distracted by the woman at the counter to notice. Unable to look any of Lanie's victims in the eye, I retrieved my sister and rolled the luggage back to its rightful owner. Then I held her hand until Mom was finished.

I couldn't blame Lanie entirely. Even though it rubbed me the wrong way, I understood how she could act so carefree. Lanie was half my age. The sleight-of-hand trick Mom was pulling might've worked on me, too, when I was six.

Look away from our family's ruin and focus on the trip to Florida! It's the Sunshine State—sadness is an impossibility! Forget that our lives are in pieces—we're going to the beach!

Right.

Getting from Tampa to Anna Maria Island required a trip over the Sunshine Skyway Bridge. As Mom drove up the steeply rising arch, Lanie sucked in her breath, then let out a noise that was halfway between a song and a sigh. The road appeared as though it paved the way to blue sky and cotton-ball clouds. The bright-yellow stabilizing cables dazzled like rays of light outside the car windows.

The dreamy expression on Lanie's face told me that she'd already ridden the bridge through the clouds and that her thoughts were somewhere high above the earth's atmosphere.

Even Mom's face brightened for a breezy second at the view. I'll admit, there was a tug at the corners of my lips, too. But it wasn't strong enough to counter the weight in my stomach. It might've been from fear—the bridge was super high. Mostly, though, I think it came from missing Dad already.

I missed the history lesson he always gave as we drove over the bridge. He called them "Forrester Family Fabulous Facts," although I might've been the only other Forrester in the family to enjoy them. As we reached the highest point, I could practically hear his annual lecture playing in my head:

The Sunshine Skyway Bridge is the longest cable-stayed concrete bridge in the world, girls. Not the first bridge to span the Tampa Bay, though. The first bridge met Disaster. Disaster with a capital D! In 1980, a freighter plowed into it during a thunderstorm. More than one thousand feet of the bridge plummeted into the bay, killing thirty-five motorists and passengers.

Disaster. That was exactly what this vacation would be without Dad. Nothing close to the magnitude of a bridge collapsing, of course, but disaster nonetheless.

Dad made everything more interesting. At his office at the university, he had an Albert Einstein quote hanging above his desk: ONCE YOU STOP LEARNING, YOU START DYING. He said he wanted to make sure that never happened to Lanie and me.

Some things he just knew, and some facts he looked up on the spot. Like when we saw a pod of dolphins, he pulled up info on his phone about their migration patterns. And when we saw a sea turtle, he pulled up images. "Okay, Olivia Forrester," he'd say, as if I were a contestant on a game show. "Name that species: loggerhead, green sea turtle, or hawksbill?"

I couldn't imagine an entire summer without his quizzes and Forrester Family Fabulous Facts. Instead of coming with us this year, he'd be teaching history classes to college students. I never imagined I'd be jealous of anyone going to summer school.

Then there was Dad's new apartment—one couch, a single chair in the kitchen, and no TV yet. I imagined him coming home to it, all quiet and empty, after a day of teaching. He had to be sad and lonely.

Grandma and Grandpa were waiting outside their beach house as we pulled into the driveway an hour later. Beads of sweat dotted the patch of wrinkled skin above Grandpa's eyeglasses, and Grandma was fanning herself with a folded piece of paper.

Every June, my mom's parents greeted us in front of their turquoise-colored home, a soaring three-story barrier between us and the beach. When we exited the car, they enveloped us in hugs and a cloud of Grandma's overly sweet perfume. They said what they always say: "Oh my word, how you girls have grown!"

There were slight differences, though—things Lanie didn't pick up on but I did. My grandparents held Mom a tad tighter and a fraction of a minute longer than usual. For the first time ever, Grandma didn't comment on how much I resemble my father.

"Grandma! Grandpa!" Lanie said. She tugged our grandmother out of her embrace with Mom by the back of her sleeveless blouse. "Look!" Lanie pointed to the pink hole in her bottom gum, and our grandparents peered in as if they'd uncovered the eighth wonder of the world. Everyone made a huge fuss over the lost tooth while ignoring the fact that Dad wasn't there.

I turned away from the group, unable to feign interest in my sister's dental development, and saw Aiden standing on the front lawn of the Beachcomber Inn next door. He was taller than last summer, and his hair was different. Longer. He wore new glasses. As good as it was to see my summer friend, my legs felt wobbly as I walked toward him. He had to have noticed my dad was missing, and I dreaded explaining why. I didn't know what to do with my hands, so I waved quickly, then shoved them into my pockets.

Aiden's grandfather was the caretaker at the inn, and Aiden

had been visiting since we were both in diapers. He had always been quiet yet playful. He inserted funny faces into conversations instead of words. He cracked jokes after barely saying anything for hours. A thousand times, he'd snuck up on me just to give me a fright.

I thought our friendship might be the one normal thing left about Florida. I stuck my tongue out, trying to initiate our usual banter, and immediately regretted it. Instead of twisting his features around or mimicking me like I expected, he tipped his head questioningly. He knew me well enough to know something was wrong.

I couldn't escape Dad's absence. It was hovering over me even now, making my reunion with Aiden as uncomfortable as everything else. At least Aiden smiled. When he did, his lopsided grin revealed smooth, straight white teeth. No more braces. It was then that I realized how much older he looked this summer.

I felt instantly self-conscious about the purple plastic headband I'd borrowed from Lanie and the lacy frills on my sleeves. The one-year age difference between Aiden and me had always seemed meaningless before. In that moment, though, I felt embarrassingly young standing in front of him.

"Hi," I said, then shifted my gaze to the inn behind him. Apparently, this was the summer for drastic changes. "Wow.

The Beachcomber looks so . . . different," I muttered, thankful it gave me something to talk about other than my absent father.

I could tell Aiden was still wondering what was up with me and my family, but he was too polite to ignore my comment. He rotated, causing the frame of his body to expand while he glanced at the Beachcomber behind him. His broadening shoulders made his torso seem more kite shaped than the beanpole he'd always been. "I know," he said. "The grand reopening was last weekend. Grandpa's new boss"—a dark expression clouded his face—"remodeled the entire property over the winter."

"Oh" was all I could think to say.

When Aiden squared his shoulders back toward me, his eyes darted to where my mom and grandparents were gathered around Lanie. I knew exactly what he wanted to ask. Before he had the chance, I blurted, "I should get back. I haven't seen my grandparents since last summer. They probably want to hear all about my year. Catch up later?"

"Sure," he said.

I could hear the disappointment in his voice, but I averted my gaze again so I wouldn't have to see it in his eyes.

As I walked away, he called out, "I'm glad you're here, Olivia."

I turned my head and smiled weakly at him. "Thanks."

I hoped things would feel less strange indoors. They didn't.

My family trailed in behind me. Lanie insisted on going to the beach right away and dragged Mom out the back door with her. Grandma drifted close, chattering away as Grandpa took multiple trips to lug in all our baggage. "Did you drink enough water on your way here, Olivia? I always seem to get dehydrated when I travel." She didn't wait for my answer before filling me a glass with water from the fridge and plowing right along.

"What were your grades like this year? All As, I bet. You're such a stellar student." While Grandma circled around me, she was unnaturally smiley. "Did you notice the renovation next door? The Beachcomber had gotten to be such an eyesore. It rarely filled, but now they're having to turn away vacationers. Oh, and did your mom tell you? Cousin Gertrude has a suspicious mole on her left shoulder."

Grandma was a retired dermatologist, so updates on other people's skin conditions were a common occurrence. As she blabbered on, I replayed the conversation I'd had with Aiden in my head. I shouldn't have left so abruptly. Maybe I should've explained about my dad. My hand shot up to the stupid plastic headband I was wearing, and I remembered the look on Aiden's face when I stuck my tongue out at him. A nervous giggle bubbled in my throat and I grimaced at the same time. Grandma halted her story to say, "I don't see how squamous cell carcinoma is funny."

I shook my head. "It's not," I said solemnly. The day was getting to me. All this pretending everything was normal and fine was exhausting. I was afraid the slightest little thing might cause me to dissolve into tears. But I couldn't lose it now. If I did, we might all fall like dominoes.

I'd never seen Mom look so pale or Dad so severe as when they'd sat Lanie and me down to break the news. Divorce. The blow was like nothing I'd felt before. Even though a few weeks had passed since they'd told us, the pain was still ricocheting in my bones.

It was behind us, though. We'd made it to Florida. I wouldn't let my family down by ruining the trip. "I'm going to check on Mom and Lanie," I said. "See what they're up to."

Grandma nodded her head, and I bolted for the back door.

Mom was standing at the edge of the surf. Lanie was chasing, and letting herself be chased, by the waves. Satisfied they were having fun, I retreated indoors. As soon as I reached my room on the top floor, I pulled out my phone. There were so many things I could've texted.

Dad, I miss you soooo much!

Are you doing okay?

Maybe even: *Why is this happening to us?*

I settled for: *We made it.*

He immediately texted back with emojis. Thumbs-up. Dolphin. Smiley face with sunglasses. Apparently, words were hard for him, too, right now.

As miserable as I felt, how much worse was this summer going to be for him? He was all on his own.

Before we left, Dad told me to "have fun."

"Sure," I'd answered unconvincingly.

"Look, I don't want you to waste your summer because of a decision your mom and I made. Go. Do what you enjoy. Learn new things. Then tell me all about it." He'd always loved summers in Florida. I made a mental note to send photos whenever I could.

The rest of the afternoon was spent unpacking. Then, after dinner, my mom and grandparents sat around talking politics and telling stories about people I'd never met. I was bored to death, but Mom frowned when Lanie wiggled out of her chair and made a break for the TV. So I stayed.

While I listened to Grandma recount her childhood, I did my best to smile even though I secretly craved time to myself. Time to *be* myself without having to worry about how my mood would affect everyone around me.

When my family finally went to bed, I tiptoed down the two flights of stairs and out the back door. The night air nearly choked me. It was so thick. The moisture coated my throat and felt heavy in my lungs. It was way different from the thin air back home.

Once I got used to it, I gulped it in greedily. I tipped my head back and let the ocean breeze wash over me. I listened to the waves and bathed in the moonlight. My chest had been tight for days. But now . . . outside by the ocean, I could finally breathe.

I wound my way down the path until I found the spot where Dad and I used to gaze at constellations and count the stars. It was just a small cutout—a place between dunes and wild grasses where the sand was soft and sheltered. I settled in and peered up. I found the three brightest stars in the eastern sky and traced the Summer Triangle with my finger. But I couldn't make out any of the constellations they belonged to—I couldn't recall their names without Dad here to remind me.

The stars weren't as bright as I'd remembered, but the number of them still made me feel small. Small and alone. I missed Dad, for sure. But I also missed what our family was before. Complete. Balanced. Mom and Lanie on one side. Me and Dad on the other. There was a natural divide down the middle. We hadn't ever talked about it, but it was there.

Mom and Lanie were the creatives, the free spirits. They were spontaneous.

Dad and I were analyzers. We made plans, and we overthought everything.

The four of us had fit together perfectly somehow. At least it'd seemed that way to me. I found four stars in the sky, making the shape of a square, and assigned one to each of my immediate family members. I covered one of the stars with my thumb. With Dad missing, I didn't fit, either—without my father's star, the square became an L. Mom and Lanie still had each other, but on the other side was only me. It felt wobbly and lopsided. I'd have to work extra hard to stay connected to them. And what about all the things I'd have to give up? Dad said to do what I enjoyed, but there was no one to plan trips to the pier or get excited about a wildlife tour with—things Lanie and Mom had zero interest in doing.

My thoughts turned to Aiden. Maybe . . . maybe he could balance things out a little. But, like everything else, he'd changed. Would he even want to hang out with me anymore? What if he thought my interests were stupid and childish now? And I still hadn't explained to him what was going on with my family.

Rising to my feet, I made my way toward the property next door. The renovations to the back of the inn were more drastic than those out front. It had been freshened with a new coat of paint. The landscaping had been redone; the pool had been spruced up; and new beach chairs, umbrellas, and cabanas had been added. It almost looked like an entirely new resort. There were too many changes for me to take in all at once. And everything was so . . . bright.

When I turned away from the lights illuminating the stairway and pool area, spots of color dotted my view. Looking at the inn had wrecked my night vision. I stumbled a few steps toward the ocean, blinking until my vision cleared. Then I blinked a few more times until I realized the dark shadow in the waves wasn't going away as my eyesight returned.

It took me a few seconds to figure out what I was seeing. A rush of excitement came over me when I did. It was a sea turtle! Its heart-shaped shadow coasted just below the surface. Its bulbous head bobbed above the waves. One flipper sent a tiny ocean spray into the night air.

For a moment, the world felt okay again. Not things-back-to-normal okay, but okay in the sense that I knew wonderful things still existed and life would bring joyful surprises when I least expected them.

I ran to the surf and slipped out of my sandals and into the frothy waves lapping the beach. The salt water stung my bare skin, just a little. It ebbed and flowed and ebbed again as my toes squished in the dampened sand, and I waded toward the gliding form. I knew better than to get too close, but I had to see. Was it a loggerhead? A green sea turtle? A hawksbill?

I couldn't Google it the way Dad would've. My parents had dumbed down my cell phone—no internet, because they thought I was too young to be "consumed" by it. But if I snapped a photo and sent it to Dad, he would be able to tell.

I barely managed to take a picture before the turtle dipped and disappeared into the deep. The photo turned out slightly blurry. And, without the moon and stars, it was a little dark, too. At least the outline of the turtle was clear, and I knew Dad would think the sighting extraordinary.

I hit send on my phone, feeling another surge of excitement. When he responded immediately with *Awesome!!! A loggerhead! So glad you're having a good time!* I knew the moment had lifted his spirits, too.

I can do this, I thought to myself. *I can move on like nothing happened. I can bury the pain.* My family had enough to worry about. If I could act cheerful, they wouldn't have to worry about me, too. If I could pretend I was happy, I knew it would make my parents happy. Then we'd all be okay, wouldn't we?

2

The largest living hard-shelled turtle
in the world is the loggerhead sea turtle.

I overslept. I couldn't help it. I only woke when Lanie slipped a note under my door. Ever since she'd started first grade, she'd been obsessed with lists. I knew her top three flavors of ice cream: cake batter, strawberry, and cookie dough; her five favorite colors, in order: yellow, purple, turquoise, mango orange, and cotton-candy blue; her seven favorite books; and her ten favorite animals. I'm not sure I even knew those things about myself.

I retrieved the piece of paper and opened it up.

Things with Shells:
1. Nuts
2. Clams

3. Eggs
4. Olivia

I glanced at the time on my phone and groaned. It was already almost noon. No wonder Lanie thought I was acting like, what? A turtle hiding in a shell. She was always doing that—pointing out similarities between things that, to me, seemed worlds apart. She'd compare snowdrifts to ocean waves and hear music in the rustle of leaves. Dad said once it was because "she has an artist's soul, like your mother."

When I'd cocked an eyebrow and smirked at that—something I'd seen him do to Mom a hundred times before, he chuckled and added, "Not exactly our forte. We prefer things that are more concrete, like facts and figures." Then he lightly bumped my shoulder.

I hurried downstairs and found Mom and Lanie on their way out to build a sandcastle on the beach. "Hey there, sleepyhead," Mom said, and asked if I wanted to join them. I didn't feel like it, but I said yes anyway.

Back in the fall, Dad and I worked up a design for a multistory creation with spiraled staircases and pointed spires. We drew the plans for our dream sandcastle on a long white paper roll. I stashed the roll in my closet next to my flip-flops and summer clothes, but when I'd found out Dad wasn't coming this year, I'd left it at home.

Mom and Lanie piled mounds of sand close to the water but far enough from the surf that they wouldn't wash away. I sat down next to them and stared out at the ocean.

After a few minutes of Mom and Lanie doing all the scooping and molding, Mom said, "Earth to Liv. We could use your help."

I snapped into action. "Here, Lanie, I can do that," I said, and she happily surrendered her shovel to me and started playing with a bucket in the water.

"Not too far," Mom told Lanie. Then to me, she said, "I really should've gotten her into swim lessons this past spring, but everything was so crazy . . ."

"I can teach her," I said, then without thinking blurted out, "Dad taught me."

Mom's lips rolled inward, her brow furrowed, and her eyes blinked a little too rapidly. "Um, we'll see . . ."

Feeling bad for reminding Mom about the past, I threw myself into shoveling sand. The thing was, once I got into it, everything else sort of melted away. I could remember enough of the plan Dad and I came up with. And as I focused in, adding details and dimension to what Lanie and Mom had started, it transformed into something amazing. It was going to be the best sandcastle we ever made.

Until Lanie ruined it.

Just as I was adding the final touches, my sister ran back with her bucket. "It needs a moat!" she cried, and poured way too much water. She may have inherited Mom's gift for imagination, but her artistic skills were lagging. Mom tried to salvage the castle by dragging her finger through the sand and creating swirly designs up the sides. But I didn't want a moat and swirls. I wanted what Dad and I had dreamed up—a dramatic castle, not a fanciful one.

Staring at Mom and Lanie's re-creation, I felt a flicker of irritation. The sandcastle Dad and I had spent so much time planning would never be built.

I mumbled something about being thirsty and needing a glass of water, then left before they noticed my disappointment. I didn't want to spoil it for Lanie and Mom, too. They were obviously pleased with the transformation. As I walked away, Lanie was wondering aloud if adding seashells would make good bathtubs for the fairies that would inhabit the castle.

To distract myself from my thoughts, I checked my phone as soon as I was back inside. Dad had texted while I was out on the beach. *How has your day been? What did you do?*

What if I were honest? What if I said that things weren't the same? That I felt like I was crumbling inside? I knew exactly what would happen. Dad would call Mom. They'd both be upset. They'd fight. And it would be my fault.

So, I took a deep breath and typed. *Great! We built a sandcastle.*

Nice! I'd love to see a photo. He fired back.

I steeled myself to go back outside to take one but, by the time I'd gotten it together, Mom and Lanie were coming in. Mom wanted to take a nap, and my grandparents were running errands, so I spent the rest of the afternoon entertaining Lanie.

Later that night, after I thought everyone had gone to bed, I snuck outside again. I wasn't twenty steps from the landing when my feet were nearly swept out from under me.

"Liiiiiiivvv!" Lanie cried as she wrapped herself around my lower torso. My sister never stopped moving. She was like a pinball—constantly knocking into people and objects around her.

I peeled her off my legs. "Why are you out here, Lanie? Go back inside."

Unfazed, she skip-hopped to investigate something in the sand a few feet away. If I were into lists the way Lanie was, I might record all the "un" words that described my sister:

1. Unfazed
2. Undaunted
3. Unworried
4. Undeterred

When Mom and Dad told us about the divorce, Lanie's biggest concern had been whether her stuffed sloth and favorite pillow could come along when we stayed at Dad's new apartment—like all shared custody meant was never-ending sleepovers.

"Liv, Liv, come quick! It's a ghost crab!" Lanie's voice surged with delight.

My head popped up. Part of me wanted to propose a hunt, like the ones Dad and I went on a couple of times each summer. We could grab flashlights. I could scoop Lanie's hand in mine, and we could stay up late searching for sinkholes in the sand and wispy tracks across the beach.

Without realizing it, I took a few steps in Lanie's direction. I stopped myself. "I *said* go inside, Lanie. Mom doesn't want you out here after dark." Mom probably wanted both of us to stay inside at night, unless we were with an adult. I caught my bottom lip between my teeth and bit down gently. How upset would Mom be if she knew I was sneaking out at night? But I needed this time to myself nearly as much as I needed air to breathe, or food to eat. It felt like a necessity.

My sister was still ignoring me as she scrambled farther down the beach in pursuit of the skittering crab.

"Lanie, get back here!"

I tore after my sister and caught her by the straps of her yellow ribbed tank top.

"Let me go!" she whined, wriggling and twisting, trying to pull away.

"Nuh-uh," I said. "You're going back to the house."

She pleaded with me. She squirmed and stretched out her shirt. I held tight, then gave one sharp tug backward. Upright again, she rocketed around, forcing the straps out of my hand. She scrunched her face and jutted her chin. She looked exactly like Mom does when she gets mad. Same wild and wavy, golden-blond hair, puffed out even more by the humidity. Same gray-green eyes.

I crossed my arms and stared her down. I must've looked like Dad in that moment. Same pale skin. Same slant to the bridge of my nose. Same pointy chin. Same brown eyes and dull-brown hair. And in every single cell, a thin streak of stubborn that came out now and then—most definitely now. I stood there unmoved, unflinching, unyielding—reveling in my own list of "un" words—until she finally relented.

"Fine!" she said.

"Fine," I said.

She marched across the beach, kicking up sand with her heels and tossing angry glances over her shoulder every few feet. I trailed her long enough to see that she'd made it inside and hadn't tried to slip away only to sneak up on me again. Then I found my way to my spot between the dunes and planted myself there.

As my stubbornness waned, I felt guilty for shooing Lanie away. But it was for the best, wasn't it? Lanie couldn't swim and she was what Dad called a "loose cannon." I couldn't keep an eye on her near the ocean when I was barely keeping myself together.

Absently, I combed my hands through the sand. A cool, hard object sank into my right palm as the sand sifted through my fingers. When I glanced down to find a piece of sea glass, frosty green and sparkling in the moonlight, the crevice in my heart cracked open a hair's breadth wider.

When sailors drown, mermaids cry, and their tears wash ashore. I could hear Dad's voice in my head. I pictured him, not as I'd seen him a few days ago, but the way he'd looked when he was here last summer—all bookish, pale knobby knees and red, sunburned shoulders. I pictured him plucking the "mermaid tears" from the beach and surrendering them to my already-overflowing pockets.

This sea glass, or mermaid tear, was tumbled and rounded by the ocean. I rubbed it between my thumb and fingers. A thin film of dried salt water and sand coated the glass. It had that unique, crusty feel that only something coughed up by the sea has.

The glass had once been a bottle or jar, discarded into the ocean, battered and lost for who knew how long before returning to land. The weight of it in my palm made my heartache and longing worse.

I buried my feelings, or at least I tried to, as I stared out at the endless water on the horizon. Mom and Lanie's sandcastle cast a curious shadow on the beach between me and the ocean. I remembered the photo Dad had asked for and dragged myself to my feet. Had he been disappointed I never sent one? I could try now, but I worried there wasn't enough light. And when I pulled out my phone, the moon disappeared behind a cloud, making the sky grow even darker.

As I was lamenting the terrible conditions for snapping a photo, a strip of illuminated water caught my attention. Something about that seemed off. If the moon was hidden, where was the light coming from? I turned my head and followed the peculiar ray shining on the surf. It was coming from the Beachcomber. The renovated inn was so bright its light was extending across the waves.

As I followed the beam back to the ocean's edge, I saw her. A sea turtle, possibly the same one I'd spotted the night before, was slowly crawling from the surf directly in front of me.

"Oh," I whispered, releasing the weight of my troubles with a single breath. Seeing the turtle had a way of doing that for me. Then I watched in soundless awe as the turtle dragged herself forward. I'd seen the roped-off areas on the island every summer. I knew sea turtles came ashore to nest from May until October. She was coming to make a nest—she had to be.

She was amazing. Lugging her heavy body across the beach with flippers made for water seemed a herculean feat. Tire-like tracks appeared in the sand behind her. Cheering her on inside my head, I willed her forward.

But a short distance in, her head began to bob. It weaved side to side. She gently veered to the left and then to the right. Then, for some reason, she stopped moving forward. Something was wrong.

I desperately wished I could help. She wanted to make a nest, didn't she? So why was she stopping? I tried to think of a way to coax her forward, a way to let her know it was safe. But nothing came to me.

Scanning the beach and our surroundings, I found nothing out of place. The light coming from the Beachcomber would have illuminated any threats. Something jogged in my memory—something Dad had said about turtles and light, but I couldn't quite recall what it was.

Before I could figure out why she seemed scared to continue, the turtle pivoted her body with one flipper until she faced the ocean again. Then she retreated into the water. I might've been imagining it, but as light shone on her face and shadows gathered in the crevices around her eyes, she looked sadder than sad. And with the waves that swallowed her whole, my own feelings of despair came crashing back.

3

Loggerhead turtles eliminate excess ocean salt
through glands located behind each eye.
When on land, the glands can make it appear
as though the turtle is crying.

The first thing that popped into my head when I woke
the next the morning was the image of the turtle
retreating—and waking with a sinking feeling is never a
good way to start the day. But I rallied. I had no other choice. I
needed to get myself downstairs before I was missed and Lanie
started mentioning my "shell" again.

Still rubbing sleep from my eyes, I went looking for everyone. I bumped into Grandma on the staircase first. She told me
(her voice laced with horror and utter disapproval) that Mom
had forgotten to reapply sunscreen on Lanie and herself while
they were working on the sandcastle. They were staying indoors
to keep the pink skin from turning red. Sure enough, when I
made it to the family room, it reeked of aloe vera.

I stopped in the middle of the archway connecting the hallway to the family room, wondering if Lanie was angry with me about our fight on the beach the night before. And if she'd mentioned it to Mom. I stood still, waiting for her to catch my gaze. When she did, it was a barely a glance. Lanie was an expert marksman when it came to shooting daggers from her eyes—but there was none of that.

My sister was caught up in her own, unrattled dream world—singing songs to herself and making lists. Our argument appeared to have been forgotten.

Mom was talking on her phone. I couldn't gauge her mood. She'd gotten good—better than me—at hiding her emotions. Mom's cheeks and the tip of her nose were ruddy from the sun, but she was still pretty—pretty in the same, unfussy way Lanie was. As I drew closer, I caught a few words of the conversation she was having. "He does travel a lot . . . I know living closer to family would make things easier . . . but the girls, I—" When she noticed me listening in, Mom cut herself off. "Can we continue this later, Michelle? I gotta go."

Mom lowered her cell and said, "Hi, sweetie!" with a tad too much enthusiasm. Before I could ask what she and my aunt had been talking about, Lanie pulled a delicate-looking shell from her pocket and began whispering into the mouth of the cream-colored cylinder.

When Lanie caught me staring, she said, "It's my wishing shell!"

"Okay," I said evenly, trying to pretend I wasn't a smidge envious. How had Lanie found such a perfect shell? It was called a lettered olive. Dad had taught me many shell names: lion's paw, coquina, conch. Some I had forgotten, but not the lettered olive. It was my favorite. "A lettered olive for Olivia," he'd say every time we came across one.

"When I whisper my wishes inside, they *have* to come true," Lanie added dreamily.

"Don't count on it," I grumbled.

Mom exhaled slightly and said, "Olivia."

A few months ago, I might've rolled my eyes at the correction. Now I sputtered an apology and, as sweetly as I could, told Lanie it was a very nice shell.

Then I waited a pause before asking, "Can we go somewhere today? It might be fun to visit the aquarium." What I didn't say was that I couldn't stop worrying about a turtle I'd seen on the beach the night before and that I was hoping to find answers there. I'd given it more thought, and I was pretty sure we'd been walking through the aquarium's sea turtle exhibit when Dad told me about the light thing. Going to the aquarium wasn't Mom's or Lanie's favorite thing to do, but it was an indoor activity, so at least it wouldn't worsen their sunburns.

"Sorry, Liv, I'm pretty wiped out." Mom stretched her arms above her head, then added, "Maybe another day?" But she didn't sound like she meant it.

So we pretty much did nothing all day. Which can be super tiring, too. Especially when you're trying to pretend you're not worried about the way your mom picks at her food and hardly eats anything. When you know your dad doesn't want to see photos of the inside of your grandparents' beach house, but you have nothing else to send him. And when your thoughts are plagued by the sad look in a sea turtle's eye, and you can't do anything about it.

I thought about calling Dad to ask about the turtles and the light, but I knew he'd hear the worry in my voice. It was one thing to fake cheerfulness in text messages, but there was no way I could pull off a lighthearted conversation—not with him, not now.

Later that night, I returned to the beach and my favorite spot between the dunes. When I let my hands drift to my sides, I found it. In the same exact spot as the night before, my fingers sifted another mermaid tear from the sand. Wonder and awe blossomed in my heart. Sea glass rarely washed ashore on Anna Maria Island. Finding a second mermaid tear felt somehow magical.

Here was another piece of sea glass, frosty and round like

the first, and it felt significant. Like a sign or something. Like maybe somewhere deep in the ocean, mermaids were weeping just for me.

But that was silly.

Almost as silly as Lanie whispering wishes into a shell.

I slipped the mermaid tear into my pocket, and it wasn't long before sleep started edging in on me. My eyelids felt heavy. The sound of the crashing waves was hypnotic. When a hand tapped my shoulder, I startled so hard I nearly screamed.

"I didn't mean to scare you," Aiden said sheepishly as I swiveled toward him. I stared in awkward silence, absorbing all the changes for a second time. It wasn't like with my grandparents. For the most part, they looked the same year after year. Aiden usually grew a few inches while we were apart. But this summer . . . this giant transformation . . . it was too much. It felt like he'd sprinted ahead of me, and the gap between us was larger than it'd ever been before.

He squirmed under my scrutiny. I couldn't be certain he was blushing—the darkness cloaked his skin in a film of gray—but I suspected he was, and that at least was comforting.

"Hey," I said. "You're back already." Aiden and his mom visited the Beachcomber and his grandfather infrequently throughout the summer. I never knew when he might show up.

Aiden's eyes flicked to the empty spot next to where I was

seated. If anyone liked listening to Dad's stories as much as I did, it was Aiden. He'd never known his own father. I think that might've been one reason he liked hanging around us so much. He had to be dying to know why Dad wasn't here, but now he seemed afraid to ask. I had acted pretty flighty before. The problem was, I still didn't know if I was ready to tackle such a difficult conversation.

"Have a seat," I said, and scooched over to make room beside me in the sand. I think we were both more at ease once we were facing the ocean, instead of making eye contact. For a little bit, anyway—until the silence became uncomfortable.

He began fiddling with a Rubik's Cube he'd brought along. The clicking and movement of his fingers was familiar and soothing. He'd started cubing last summer. He was so proud when he showed Dad and me that he knew how to solve the puzzle. Not that Aiden was one to brag—I could just tell. He'd tried to teach me a few algorithms he'd learned on YouTube— and I'd gotten to a point where I could unscramble the first few layers—but then summer ended. I regretted not practicing at all during the school year.

"You've gotten faster," I said when each of the six sides showed only one color. There was something appealing about it. A random mess of red, green, orange, yellow, blue, and white squares being sorted and arranged neatly. It made me wish that when life got mixed up, it could be unjumbled—that it was possible for everything to be clicked back into place.

"Thanks. New speed cube. It's smoother," Aiden said.

"Cool."

"Want to scramble it for me?" he asked.

I took the cube and started twisting and turning the layers until the colors were all mixed up again. I wanted to apologize for bolting the day I'd arrived, and I knew I should explain my father's absence, but the words wouldn't form inside my head, let alone exit my mouth. I handed the cube back to Aiden. He took it but didn't attempt another solve. He seemed to be waiting for me to say something.

When I stayed clammed up, he said, "Where's your—"

I had to think of something to say, and quick. "I saw a sea turtle here last night and the night before that," I blurted before he could finish his sentence.

For a moment I worried I might as well have been wearing a cartoon princess T-shirt—that my love of sea turtles would make me seem silly and young. But then he said, "That's great." His response struck me as genuine, but also a tad disappointed. I'd brought up the turtle as a diversion, and we both knew it.

I continued anyway. "Yeah . . ." I hedged. "Except . . .

except she started crawling ashore last night, but turned around before making a nest. I think . . . I think all the light coming from the Beachcomber might've scared her away."

"Hmm," Aiden said. "But you're not sure?"

I shook my head.

"Wouldn't your, um, dad know?" he asked in a voice so soft I could barely hear him over the crashing surf.

I shook my head, harder this time. Dad would know, but I didn't want to go there.

"Olivia, why—"

I cut Aiden off before he could finish. "Maybe your grandfather can help. He can turn off the lights at night, can't he? Will you ask him for me?"

Aiden searched my face, then quickly dropped his gaze. "No," he said, as if he were speaking to the sand.

His answer surprised me. It wasn't like Aiden to tell me no. When we were younger, he'd let me wrap him in capes made from seaweed and would pretend to be anyone I wanted him to be—my co-explorer, an evil villain, or an alien from a distant planet.

"Please, I'm really worried about—" I started.

"No."

He cut *me* off this time. I knew I was acting differently, but why was he? Our friendship had always felt so natural and easy. Maybe he wasn't interested in being my friend anymore. He had other friends he could hang out with this summer. I didn't. I didn't really have anyone else to turn to.

"But—"

"Look, you don't even know that the Beachcomber *is* the problem," he grumbled.

I opened my mouth to speak again, then closed it without saying another word. It crossed my mind that he might be shutting me out because that's what I was doing to him. But I'd never known Aiden to be petty. Last summer I would've pressed him for a reason. Then again, last summer there were no secrets between us. I let it go, and we fell back into silence. I didn't get sleepy again—not with Aiden beside me. Even the thought of having thoughts was draining, though, so I let my mind go blank. I let myself be lulled into sweet nothingness by the night.

4

**Loggerheads are carnivorous.
They use their strong jaws and sharp beaks
to crush the shells of crabs and shrimp.**

Grandpa stood at the counter, dressed in a checkered robe, grinding coffee beans. When he noticed my arrival, he spun around to greet me. "Good morning, Olivia." There was a playful twinkle in his eye as he held up the bag of beans. "Precise grinding enhances the flavor and aroma, but I suppose you're too young to appreciate coffee."

I shrugged. That was sort of true. Dad had lent me sips from his mug before. It always singed my mouth and tasted bitter. But the smell was another story. The smell reminded me of our local bookstore back in Denver. It reminded me of rain, Saturday mornings, and a cool breeze wafting through open windows. It reminded me of Dad and home and made my knees feel weak. "It's okay," I said.

He nodded and went back to work.

"Um, Grandpa . . ."

He released his finger, and the burr of the grinder came to a halt. "Yes, dear?"

"Do you think we can go to the aquarium today?"

"Well, I don't see why not. Always a good time, seeing the dolphins and the sharks, and—I imagine your mom and sister will want to come, too."

I shook my head. "I don't think so. Lanie gets grossed out by the eels, and I asked Mom yesterday and she didn't seem interested."

Grandpa took off his glasses and wiped them on his shirt. He was stalling as he gave it some thought. This was one of the reasons I'd singled out Grandpa. He mulled things over, but never really pried. He left rapid-fire inquisitions to Grandma.

"I suppose that would be all right," he said, returning the glasses to his face. "Just give me a minute while I get dressed and leave a note."

I smiled to myself as he left the room. We were headed to the aquarium!

It ate at me that Aiden hadn't been willing to ask his grandfather for help, but he'd been right about one thing: I wasn't positive the Beachcomber *was* the reason the turtle had turned away. Before I asked Mr. Emerson to shut off the inn's lights, I'd need to be certain they were the culprit.

Whatever Forrester Family Fabulous Fact that Dad had shared with me about sea turtles and lighting was after he'd read a sign at the turtle exhibit. I was sure of it. Plus, I could snap a photo or two for Dad while we were there.

Grandpa and I arrived early. So early, the aquarium wasn't open yet. This never would've happened with Dad. Dad always had a perfectly planned itinerary, with opening times and coupons to boot. I peered in the darkened windows, feeling my pulse start to rise. I was angry with myself for not doing Dad's job—for not calling ahead. At least I knew exactly where the turtle exhibit was. I'd make a beeline as soon as the doors opened.

"Ah, Olivia," Grandpa said, watching me. "You're so very focused."

I turned my head. Mom had told me the same thing zillions of times, but when Grandpa said it, it didn't sound like an insult and it wasn't followed with an exasperated "just like your father."

"It's a wonderful quality, but some of the best adventures happen when you deviate from the plan." Grandpa winked mischievously. "Shall we walk around a little? Come back when it's open?"

I shrugged, then nodded reluctantly. "I guess so."

Grandpa flashed me a crooked smile and shot off with devilish speed for a man his age. I couldn't keep up as he wandered across the street over to the bay side and down to the marina.

He was talking to a college-aged girl when I caught up. Sunlight shone off her dark brown skin, and she smiled broadly as I approached. "So, you must be Olivia. I understand you and your grandfather are going to give kayaking a try."

"Er . . ."

"Don't worry. You don't need any paddling experience," she said.

I searched Grandpa's face for an explanation. "Why not?" Grandpa said. "We've got time to kill, don't we?"

The next thing I knew, I'd been fitted with a wet suit, I was sitting in a narrow boat with Grandpa behind me, and I was being launched into the water. After our guide, whose name I learned was Sarah, pushed us in, she launched herself in a solo kayak.

I reached for my phone thinking Dad would love to kayak like this, and how pleased he would be to see me out doing something fun. I'd send the photo to my friends, too, of course. But Sarah cautioned, "You know, I can't tell you how many phones and cameras I've seen accidentally tossed overboard. You might want to tuck that somewhere safe." So I did.

Sarah told us she *was* a college student. She was studying to be a marine biologist and was running ecotours to help pay for school. She knew almost as much about everything as Dad did. We paddled through dark tunnels formed by scraggly trees called mangroves and glided across the still bay. The roots of the mangroves seemed perched on top of the water. Sarah said they're called "walking trees."

Despite myself, I got caught up listening as Sarah told us how many animals the mangroves provide food and shelter for—fishes, shellfish, and crustaceans. While she explained how the walking trees filter out harmful things and do so much for the overall health of Florida's coastal zone, I forgot about the aquarium and my problems. I just enjoyed the tour.

I enjoyed dipping the oar in the water, pulling it toward me, and feeling the kayak propel forward. I enjoyed sticking the paddle in the current to change directions. I enjoyed watching the treetops for signs of life and Sarah pointing out sea stars in the mangrove roots. When a big black bird submerged and swam beneath the tip of the kayak, Sarah said it was a cormorant diving for fish.

I remembered a Forrester Family Fabulous Fact and shared it with Sarah. "A cormorant can go as deep as one hundred feet to catch its prey."

She clapped her hands. "Very good! A science girl after my own heart."

I was so excited to watch the bird, the wave of sadness I felt at the thought of Dad was as light as a passing breeze.

After the tour, Grandpa and I walked back to the aquarium, talking about the sea stars and a manatee that'd lumbered by. The doors were open now, and we bought tickets. Seeing the turtle exhibit was still important. But as we walked inside, the jellyfish caught my attention. They were mesmerizing, floating like translucent clouds in the water.

I lost track of time standing by the tanks, hypnotized by their graceful, flowing movements. When I finally stepped away, Grandpa suggested we visit the shark exhibit next. I didn't mind. We learned that sharks almost never get sick and that scientists are studying them in hopes of finding ways to treat human illnesses.

Grandpa was a quieter companion than Dad. He didn't add stories and tidbits of information as we walked around, but he didn't lollygag and gab about totally unrelated things, either—the way Mom and Lanie would have. He gave me time to read signs and think thoughts without interruption. I figured the more time we spent at the aquarium, the better. I would see the turtle exhibit eventually.

We stopped by the stingray pool after we'd spent some time observing the leering hammerheads. The aquarium allowed visitors to pet the rays, with a gentle stroke using the back side of two fingers.

Time slipped away from me the same way it had while we were kayaking. It was nice to step out of my life for a day. I'd been so on edge every moment since we arrived—trying to please my mom and keep peace with Lanie. Even hanging out with Aiden the night before had felt like work. It was small wonder I could relax here, surrounded by marine animals and loads of information.

"Olivia, we need to get going," Grandpa said. "If we're going to eat at a halfway decent hour, I need to start dinner soon."

Grandpa's words shook me from my blissful daze. I withdrew my hand from the stingray pool. "Please, not yet. We haven't seen the turtles."

Grandpa glanced at his watch and nodded his head reluctantly. "All right, then. We can spare a few more minutes." As I wove through the crowd, I inwardly scolded myself. Why had I let myself be distracted? As much as I'd enjoyed meandering through the aquarium with Grandpa, I should've insisted on visiting the turtle exhibit right away.

Once we made it to the corridor I was looking for,

I discovered the aquarium had five sea turtles; three of them had been injured by boats and nursed back to health at the aquarium's rehabilitation center. Most turtles who visited the hospital were returned to the ocean. These three couldn't be because their vision was too poor. I felt a wave of pity for them, but the turtle I'd seen on the beach hadn't looked injured, so I moved on.

From the next display, I learned that a sea turtle's sex is determined by the temperature of the sand when it's still in the egg. Nests in warmer sand produce more females.

"Hurry, please, Olivia," Grandpa said.

I sped to the next sign, where I gathered that sea turtles have been swimming the oceans since the Jurassic period. They survived what dinosaurs couldn't but now faced many modern threats—hunting, loss of beaches, and trash. My stomach twisted into a ball of knots when I read that thousands of turtles die every year after eating or becoming entangled in plastic bags. They mistake the plastic bags for jellyfish.

Then I came to a placard that read WHAT YOU CAN DO, and my eyes got stuck on the very first line:

1. Turn off or shield outdoor lights

This was it—what Dad had been talking about! My throat tightened as I read on.

Artificial lighting on beaches discourages the turtles from nesting in safe places and disorients hatchlings. Hatchlings use moonlight to navigate their way to the ocean. Bright lights coming from the shoreline can confuse baby turtles and lead them astray.

Here was the answer I'd been searching for. The light coming from the Beachcomber was what was scaring the turtle away. I snapped my first photo of the day—proof!—while a whole slew of emotions washed over me—anger, frustration, sadness. I wanted to scream. Instead, I quietly scanned the rest of the display, but it was about cleaning up trash and filling in holes that could entrap hatchlings on their way to the water. It said nothing more about lighting.

Grandpa gave my upper arm a gentle squeeze. "Olivia, my dear, I'm afraid we're out of time."

I looked at him pleadingly. I wasn't ready. I wanted to talk to someone. I wanted to find out more about the artificial lighting, its effects on the sea turtles, and what could be done about the Beachcomber. I couldn't turn off the inn's lights, or shield the beach from all that illumination myself, but there had to be something someone could do to help the poor turtle.

"I'm sorry, but not only is supper going to be late, your mother is going to be worried. We've been gone a very long time."

He was right. Mom would start thinking we'd been in a car accident, or worse, if we didn't get back soon. My head drooped like it was on a rope instead of connected to my backbone. I bobbed my chin up and down obediently, then let my grandfather lead me out of the aquarium.

It wasn't until we were in the car on our way back to the beach house that realized I'd been so absorbed with what I was doing that I hadn't taken any photos worthy to share with Dad. That and my concern for the turtle cast a dark shadow on what would otherwise have been a fun day.

5

The loggerhead sea turtle's scientific name is *Caretta caretta*.

Grandpa joined Grandma in the kitchen when we returned. I wandered into the family room and found Mom on the phone and Lanie whispering into her shell. Two Popsicle wrappers lay on the glass coffee table and Mom had unpacked the Shrinky Dinks paper and the tin of seventy-two "artist quality" colored pencils. It appeared they hadn't left the house for the second day in a row.

"I know, sis, Florida will always feel like home, but—" Mom was saying into her cell.

Home. Mom's conversation jogged one of Dad's Forrester Family Fabulous Facts in my memory: *Loggerheads return to the exact beach where they were born to lay their eggs.* I connected that with what I'd learned at the aquarium, and my heart broke impossibly more. This beach, the one right outside my window, was where the sea turtle had hatched from an egg and dashed for the ocean waves. This beach was familiar to her. It was her beach. It was calling her home. Her babies were supposed to be born here, the way she was. The light from the Beachcomber was messing everything up.

Mom continued, "I'm not sure the courts would even allow that . . . And uprooting the girls might not be what's best for them. They love it here, but . . ."

What was she talking about? Mom had said something last time they were on the phone about how living closer to family would make things easier. Was Aunt Michelle trying to convince her to move to Florida? For good? My stomach leaped into my throat. But the idea was more than I could process at the moment, what with alarm bells for the sea turtle still blaring inside my head.

"Argh!" I said, and Lanie jolted.

I crouched down on the floor beside her. "It's okay. I just need to go next door quickly. I'll be right back. Don't tell anyone." By "anyone," I meant Mom. I especially didn't want to worry or upset her now. If she was toying with the idea of moving to Florida permanently, the last thing I wanted was to make things harder on her. If she thought Lanie and I were more than she could handle on her own, she might actually decide to move us to be closer to her parents and sister. Then I'd hardly ever get to see Dad.

I refused to let myself be rattled by something that may never happen. At least, not until I had the turtle situation resolved. No one, save Lanie, noticed me leaving. I lucked out in locating Mr. Emerson, too. He was outside, on a ladder, cleaning a gutter.

The way Aiden had acted the night before weighed on me as I approached his grandfather. Now that I had proof, would Aiden react differently? A part of me was scared to find out. I couldn't wait for Aiden to show up. I had to ask his grandfather now.

Mr. Emerson didn't look much like his grandson. He was stout and balding, and while Aiden often seemed out of sync with his own feet and limbs, Mr. Emerson was the type of person who appeared fully in control of every movement he made.

Aiden's grandfather didn't notice me. I stood below him a moment, and my nerves almost caused me to abandon my mission. If I didn't do anything, though, if I didn't speak up, and I saw the turtle turning away from the beach again, or worse, if she never came back, I'd be crushed.

It took far longer than it should have, but I finally mustered the courage to say, "Excuse me, please." I thought if I was extra polite, there was a better chance he'd listen.

Mr. Emerson glanced down, no doubt recognized me, and said, "Aiden's not around today, but I can tell him you stopped by next time he's here."

I shook my head. "I'm not here about Aiden . . . I'm here about . . . a turtle."

"Oh?" That seemed to pique his curiosity, but not enough for him to climb down from the gutter. "A turtle?" he asked, leaning over to get a better look at me.

"It's, well, all the light . . . from the Beachcomber . . . It's disturbing a turtle. She wants to come ashore to make a nest, but she can't because the light is scaring her off. And lights are bad for baby turtles, too. They—"

Mr. Emerson cut me off. With an entirely straight face he said, "So you've talked with this turtle, have you?"

"What? No. I—"

Mr. Emerson chuckled. "I'm sorry. I shouldn't toy with you like that."

That *did* remind me of Aiden—poking fun at me, then apologizing for it. At least, it reminded me of the *old* Aiden. But I wasn't in any mood for jokes.

"I saw her!" I shot back. "She crawled onto the sand and then turned around. It was the light! I have proof." I retrieved my phone from my pocket, clicked open the photo of the aquarium display, and held it toward him even though there was no way he could read the small lettering from his position high on the ladder.

"Okay, okay," Mr. Emerson said. "I believe you."

I'm not sure where it all came from. It wasn't like me to be so forward. A tiny part of me was appalled that I'd spoken this way to Aiden's grandfather, of all people. But a much larger part of me felt, I don't know, relief maybe? It felt good to purge a little bit of everything I'd been holding in.

"So?" I hounded. "What are you going to do about it? The lights, I mean. Can you turn them off?"

I waited patiently while Mr. Emerson climbed down from the ladder. Once he'd stepped off the bottom rung, he turned to face me. "No. I'm not going to do anything."

"Nothing?" The pride I'd felt for holding my ground whooshed right out of me.

"It's not that I don't care about the turtles," he said sadly. "Before the landscaping was redone, tree branches blocked any light that might've reached the beach. I've mentioned to Mr. Shaw . . ." Mr. Emerson met my eyes and his brow furrowed. "Mr. Shaw's my new boss, you see. Well, I've mentioned to him that we need to replace all the bulbs with turtle-friendly lighting."

"And?" I nudged.

"And Mr. Shaw doesn't feel it's a high priority. We're still in the red. We're not making money because of all the improvements. Retrofitting the outdoor lighting is expensive. It's on the list but, again, not a priority."

"Tell that to the turtle!" I huffed.

Mr. Emerson exhaled heavily. "If only Mr. Shaw—" he said, then cut himself off.

My mind inserted endings to his sentence. If only Mr. Shaw, what? Cared? Were here? Were more interested in turtles? Were less greedy?

Could Mr. Shaw be the reason Aiden hadn't wanted me to approach his grandfather? It would almost be a relief if that were true.

"Look, I don't mean to disappoint you, Olivia," Mr. Emerson said. "Honest, I don't. And I am sorry for being condescending before. When you're young, things seem so simple. So . . . black and white. Someday you'll understand that things are more complex. They don't always turn out the way you want them to. But that's life." Mr. Emerson started folding up his ladder. "Now, if you'll excuse me, I have more gutters to clean."

For as long as I lived, I didn't think I would ever feel differently about helping the turtle.

. . .

When I snuck to the beach that night, I didn't see the logger-head, but I found tracks again. Tracks that ended abruptly, not far enough inland. Tracks that stopped right in line with the ray of light coming from the Beachcomber.

A few summers before, Dad and I found the remains of a small loggerhead on the beach, tangled in seaweed. I was repulsed by the carcass but, at the same time, I couldn't look away.

"What happened to it?" I'd asked. I assumed Dad had an answer for everything back then. But he shrugged. He said only one in a thousand sea turtle hatchlings make it to adult-hood. He said what I'd read at the aquarium. That sea turtles are threatened by many things: birds, boats, predators in the ocean, people.

I'd always considered turtles invincible with their hard, protective shells. Turns out, the opposite is true. They're incred-ibly vulnerable. They face terrible odds, and most of them don't make it.

Thinking back on that day, my blood pulsed hot and my heart ached. How could sea turtles ever survive if the people who could help didn't care enough to try?

6

Unlike land turtles, sea turtles cannot retract their heads or limbs into their shells.

anie's face was three inches above mine. Her tangled curls brushed my forehead, and her warm breath felt tacky on my skin. I groaned. "You're supposed to knock." I was groggy, and sleep hadn't erased my unease about the turtle any more than my conversation with Mr. Emerson had. "Go away," I said.

"You're up!"

Through half-open lids, I could see that Lanie was pure, unbridled happiness. The pink burn on her cheeks had faded, leaving a healthy glow in its place. I pulled a pillow over my face, shielding myself from her radiance.

"Grandma said we have to wait on you for donuts. So get up!" Lanie tugged at the pillow, but I refused to let it go.

Typically, I love donuts, especially ones from the Donut Experiment, where customers build their own, choosing from a list of icings and toppings. Dad and I always passed on the rainbow sprinkles and candy and went straight for the key lime–flavored drizzle. But the thought of only checking *one* key-lime donut on the made-to-order sheet turned my stomach. And, even though I'd made a promise to myself, I wasn't up to pretending like everything was okay right then.

When Lanie gave up on yanking the pillow away, I lowered it myself. "Tell everyone I don't feel well and that I said to go without me."

"But—"

"Just tell them."

Lanie pulled back. She lifted her hand, revealing the lettered olive, whispered softly into it, then quickly vaulted off my bed. "I'll bring you one!" she shouted while clomping down the stairs.

I would've drawn the pillow back over my head, but Lanie left the door open. I rose to close it and, on my way back, grabbed my phone from the nightstand. Text messages lined the screen. A photo of my best friend Mia's new puppy. Abigail complaining about her pesky younger brother and having to babysit him all summer. Emily telling me I was "SO lucky" to be at the beach. The closest she'd come to any water activities would be "surfing Netflix."

I scrolled down and there was a text from Dad, too. *Didn't hear from you yesterday . . . You must've been too busy having fun to text your boring old dad.* ☺ *What's on the agenda for today?*

I felt a wave of guilt for forgetting to snap a better photo at the aquarium. And I didn't want to tell him that I'd passed on donuts because the thought of having one without him made me sick. *Nothing,* I typed, then quickly deleted it. *Reading.* Nope that wouldn't do, either.

I tried to think of what he'd want to hear. I quickly pecked out *Visiting the Anna Maria City Pier* and hit send before I could change my mind.

Hey! I've been wondering about that pier. Send me a photo so I can see how the repairs are coming along.

Crud. I'd forgotten that the pier had been damaged by Hurricane Irma. Of course Dad would be interested. *Too* interested.

Sure, I typed, and at the same time wondered how on earth I was going to get out of my lie. Or maybe I didn't have to . . . I could take the trolley to the pier, snap a photo, and be back before anyone missed me.

The thought of riding the trolley alone made me nervous.

Nobody had ever said it wasn't allowed, though. And I rode the bus to school on my own—this wasn't much different. But it was the type of thing I should probably get permission for. Except . . . everything was changing, and I *was* practically thirteen. With everything going on, I'd nearly forgotten that my birthday was coming up. It was less than a week away.

I was basically a teenager. I was old enough to start doing more things by myself. Maybe I could start taking the city bus when we returned home, too. Mom wouldn't have to give me so many rides, and maybe I could do some of the shopping. That would make things easier on her, wouldn't it? Then she wouldn't even consider moving to Florida.

That settled it. Riding the trolley on my own to the pier was a good idea. I could prove to myself that it wasn't a big deal, and I could take photos to send to my friends back home, too. Not just Dad. Then *everyone* would think I was having a wonderful time instead of being sad and obsessing about a turtle.

It took less than a minute to get dressed, and even less time to flit down the stairs. The house was still and quiet as I made my way toward the front door. It was so quiet, the growl from my stomach sounded like a roar. Obviously, I was hungry—just not for donuts.

There's time for a quick bite, I reasoned, and redirected my steps toward the kitchen. Grandpa calls himself a food enthusiast. He doesn't like the word *foodie*. He says it lacks sophistication and makes a person sound like a food addict rather than someone passionate about skill and proficiency in the kitchen. Grandma says the point of cooking is to provide nourishment for the family, and that Grandpa should get over himself already.

Years of disagreement had resulted in two types of foods in their kitchen. Grandma's comfort foods: cans of tomato soup, loaves of soft white bread, slices of bologna, and iceberg lettuce. And Grandpa's gourmet ingredients (which were mostly unidentifiable to me): roots of some sort, brightly colored vegetables, raw fish, and terrible-smelling cheeses.

What I wouldn't have given for a Pop-Tart.

I was riffling through the cupboard by the fridge when I heard a muffled sound coming from behind the pantry door. It struck me as the sound a wild animal might make. Mia's family owned a cabin in the Rocky Mountains. She was always telling stories about critters that found their way inside: squirrels, mice, pack rats, even marmots. I wasn't as familiar with Florida wildlife. I feared a snake or alligator might be hiding behind the door, but a harmless crab or lizard seemed much more likely.

I swung it open and . . . there stood my mother.

She had splotchy, red-spotted skin and tearstained cheeks. We stood face-to-face, frozen for what seemed like an eternity.

My mom was crying.

My mom was hiding and crying in the pantry. It brought back memories of all the times I'd caught her crying before. Too many times. Too many times, I hadn't known what to say—just like I didn't know now. I balled my hands and squeezed. "Mom," I squeaked out. "Are you okay?"

When my parents got angry with each other, I never knew how to deal with it. I never knew what was normal. It's not like I could survey Mia and Abigail. *How often do your parents argue? How loud are their fights? Does your dad ever cry when it's over? Does your mom?*

Emily's parents got divorced when we were in first grade. We'd been so young. I hadn't known what she was going through. I guess I should've asked. And Emily was far from the only person I knew whose parents had split. The *d* word was something that got tossed around all the time, but no one ever *really* talked about it. Or maybe they did, and I didn't pay close enough attention. If I had, would I have seen the divorce coming?

Now Mom was crying even though Dad wasn't here. Why? And why was she tucked away in the pantry? Had she heard me come down and hid because she didn't want me to see her like this? I didn't know where to begin sorting out what the divorce was doing to her. Even if I could understand it, I didn't know that I wanted to.

She nodded her head. "I'm sorry, Oliv-ia." My mom's voice cracked as my named rolled off her tongue. She was embarrassed—me being here, it wasn't comforting to her—it was making things worse.

Some primal instinct kicked in and I fled. My thoughts were all mixed up like one of Aiden's unsolved cubes. The ache in my chest spread, then sunk into my stomach. My vision blurred as I burst out the door, across the driveway, and sped onto the front grounds of the Beachcomber.

The only thing I could do was get away—put distance between me and all the things I couldn't control.

"Hey! Kid! Get out of the flower bed! You're crushing my hibiscus." In my peripheral vision, I saw Aiden's grandfather. My head whipped toward him. The skin of his forehead gathered in lines above his heavily hooded eyes. His scraggly gray beard and mustache surrounded tightly pinched lips. But I knew the sound of his voice, and it hadn't been the one I'd heard.

"Kid, seriously? Watch where you're going!"

I adjusted my line of sight and found another man standing on the Beachcomber's lawn. He was decades younger than Aiden's grandfather, had way more hair (at least on top of his head), and was far better dressed. It wasn't just his clothes. The man's entire appearance—from his perfectly coifed light-brown hair to his shiny black shoes—was polished and refined. He smiled at me, but it didn't feel welcoming.

"I-I'm sorry," I stammered, and kept walking. Walking toward the trolley stop. Walking away from the men. Walking away from my crying mother.

Desperate to see the top of the trolley bus wobbling above traffic, I peered down the street. Even though things on Anna Maria Island moved at a more leisurely pace than they did back home, the cars whizzed by. One by one, vehicles flew down the street.

When the trolley finally pulled to the stop, I was still so rattled I didn't notice it was headed in the wrong direction. I rode the southbound trolley all the way to Bradenton Beach before realizing my mistake. By the time I switched buses, I knew Lanie and my grandparents would be back from getting donuts. The day had barely begun and already it was a nightmare.

Once I arrived at the correct stop, I ran to the pier, whipped out my phone, pointed, and clicked. Normally, I would've taken a moment to enjoy the view, the warm morning glow and the pink-tinted clouds. Instead, I darted straight back to the street. Not that it did me any good. In all my hurry, I'd failed to consider how long it would take for another trolley to appear.

While I waited, I opened the photo app on my phone again. A text from Mom popped up on the screen—*Where are you?* I ignored it and sent the snapshot of the pier to Dad and my friends. Mia texted back first. *Wow! Beautiful.* Then Dad's reply came—*Happy to see the pier is coming along and even happier to know you're out sightseeing!* A tiny part of the weight lifted from my shoulders.

It was a small victory, but wins seemed hard to come by these days. Especially for the sea turtle. She was losing over and over, and until the lights at the Beachcomber were turned off, I didn't see how she could ever triumph. I sighed to myself. With all the things bothering me, I really didn't need to be fretting about a turtle, too. But I couldn't stop thinking about her.

It was at least fifteen minutes before the next trolley came, and I was sweating buckets when I climbed aboard. I'd run out on Mom in the middle of a breakdown. As I slid into an open seat, I pushed away thoughts of the sea turtle and went back to dreading the jam I was headed for. What was I thinking heading off on the trolley alone?

My grandparents probably freaked when they came home and Mom was in tears and I wasn't there. Sure enough, when the trolley rolled up to the stop near my grandparents' beach house, the whole family was out looking for me. Mom must've met them in the driveway, because Grandpa was holding his car keys, and the donut box was in Lanie's hands. No doubt, they'd never made it inside.

I ducked my head as soon as my feet hit the sidewalk. Lanie spotted me right away and shot toward me, carrying the box of donuts in her arms. She uttered a breathless stream of words. "Liv! Liv! I got you a key lime. What are you doing, Liv? Why weren't you here? Where did you go?"

Before I could think of an answer, she was tromping through the same flower bed I'd gone through. Mr. Emerson and the stranger were still outside, and the well-dressed man didn't seem at all happy to see his hibiscus plants getting crushed again.

"Hey!" he called, then stormed in, his face reddening as he flew toward Lanie and the flower bed. But when he saw the rest of my family standing a short distance away, he halted abruptly, straightened his tie, and combed his fingers through his hair.

It was too late. Lanie had already been spooked. She shrieked in surprise and threw the donut box up in the air. Time seemed to stand still as the box rose. The lid flew open. A dozen donuts shot out across the neatly trimmed grass.

The black cloud of birds that descended was nearly instantaneous. It was as if they'd been circling the island, just waiting for a little girl to toss donuts up in the air and for their chance to swoop in. Seagulls and sandpipers gobbled down candy toppings. They pecked holes in the frosting and threw pieces of spongy cake high and caught them with their beaks.

My sister scurried to her feet and tried to chase the birds

away. She charged at one. It floated a few feet out of reach as another one dove in.

My mom and the stranger reached Lanie first. Mom helped my sister scoop the donut remains back into the box, and the man found more success than Lanie had in shooing away the birds. By the time I got to them, there was nothing I could do but feel terrible for being the cause of such a ruckus.

Nevertheless, relief flooded Mom's eyes when she saw me. "Liv, where did you go?"

"I—" My mouth hung open, wanting to tell her about my solo ride on the trolley, and how I was old enough to take on more responsibility, but that I was also sorry because I knew I should've said something instead of leaving her there in the pantry.

Before I could gather my wits, though, the man was speaking over me. "Hi there, ladies, I'm Frank Shaw—the new owner of the Beachcomber. Say, you three must be sisters." As he said this, he cocked his chiseled cleft chin at my mother and raised one eyebrow.

I frowned. This was Mr. Shaw? As in, the Mr. Shaw who oversaw all decisions regarding the lighting of the inn? "I'm Olivia," I said, and thrust out my hand. "This is my mom and my sister, Lanie."

Mr. Shaw shook my hand but kept his eyes on my mother. "Remarkable genes in the family—beautiful bone structure."

Mom blushed, and I said, "Er, thanks," while wondering how to shift the conversation toward the sea turtle.

My grandparents joined the circle then, and Mr. Shaw said, "Wow . . . three generations of exquisite women?" then let out a low whistle. "You're a lucky man," he said to my grandfather.

Grandpa narrowed his eyes. Mr. Shaw didn't seem to be making a good impression on him. On me either, but I smiled anyway because I knew I'd need Mr. Shaw's cooperation to get the lights turned off.

"You know, I hate to ask this, but could you please tell the little ones to kindly stay out of my flower beds? The grounds were in dire need of maintenance when I acquired the property." He threw a sidelong glance at Aiden's grandfather. "We've brought things up to a much higher standard . . . But it's not easy to keep it there."

The straight line of Mr. Emerson's mouth twitched beneath his mustache. Then, as if he couldn't stand to be there another minute, Mr. Emerson turned and walked away.

Grandma nodded her head. "Of course," she said in reply to Mr. Shaw, and took Lanie by the hand. "Come on, honey." Then she shot me an expectant look. "Olivia, I'll speak to you inside."

Getting scolded by Grandma wasn't something I was

looking forward to. But even more than that, I didn't want to go inside and miss my opportunity to tell Mr. Shaw about the harmful light his inn was casting onto the beach.

Lanie sniveled and kept her eyes glued to the colorful mess and the crumpled donut box, and Grandma guided her forward. Mom turned to follow.

I steeled myself to speak. "Mr.—" I started, but then Mr. Shaw grabbed Mom by the elbow.

"Hey," he said, voice as smooth as silk. "If you'd like, I can show you around one of the units at the inn. Maybe you and your daughters would be interested in a long-term lease? Might be nice having your own space but still living next door to the folks. Am I right?"

Mom smiled pensively. "Well . . ."

I thought she was just being polite. But what if she wasn't? What if she really was considering moving into one of the units at the Beachcomber? Anna Maria Island was one of my favorite places in the world. It wasn't where I wanted to live year-round, though. I would miss the mountains and the snow, and my friends, and most of all—Dad. He'd never be able to move here with his job at the university. No matter how worried I was about the turtle, the firecrackers going off inside my head were telling me to get my mother out of there, and fast.

"Mom?" I said, gently tugging on the same bare arm

Mr. Shaw had snatched hold of a few seconds before. "Shouldn't we check on Lanie? She was pretty upset . . ."

"I'll think about it," she told Mr. Shaw. "It was nice meeting you."

"Likewise," he said in a manner that made Mom's cheeks redden again and made me want to gag.

I glanced around as Mom and I made our way back to the house. Never one to litter, Grandpa had been lingering behind. As he retrieved the box and the remaining donut crumbs, his gaze flicked to the sign for the trolley stop and then to me. His warm honey-brown eyes shone with understanding. The world felt too big in that moment, but I found myself nodding and softly smiling in his direction.

With Mom in front and Grandpa behind, there was no way for me to pull Mr. Shaw aside. I would have to talk to him about the light when the timing was better.

7

Each year, hundreds of thousands of sea
turtles are caught in fishing nets and on hooks.
Since turtles must reach the surface to breathe,
many drown once caught.

Mom stopped not one foot inside the doorway. Lanie
didn't give her a chance to move deeper inside the
house. My sister had fallen to pieces as soon as she'd
entered and was openly mourning the loss of donuts. Mom
rested her hand on Lanie's shoulder. Grandma was beside
them both with her arms crossed.

I shrank with my back against the door. I felt bad for Lanie,
but she was getting enough attention and I had things to do. I'd
missed my opportunity to confront Mr. Shaw, but when I had
another one, I wanted to be prepared. That meant planning
out what to say, maybe even putting together a science fair–
worthy project. Facts, figures, photos. Lanie was the list maker,

but she had nothing on me when it came to informational presentations.

I was antsy to get started, but my family was creating a roadblock. Still, I didn't want to be rude—especially with Lanie rightfully upset. Grandpa raised his eyebrows at me sympathetically and cleared his throat. "We know this has been a trying morning for everyone, but if you don't mind, we would like to get through," he said.

"But—" Grandma started, her eyes flicking to me with accusation.

Grandpa raised his hand like a stop sign. "One crisis at a time, dear. Let's tend to Lanie first."

Grandma considered the tears streaming down Lanie's face and relented. She and Mom scooched to one side so I could get by. My foot had just brushed the bottom step, and I thought I was all but in the clear when the front door whooshed open once more.

"Surprise!" My aunt Michelle stepped into the foyer with two dark-haired boys trailing behind her. "The MOB has arrived!"

My aunt deemed herself the "MOB" after the twins were born and had been trying to convince my mom to call herself the "MOG" ever since. MOG for *mom of girls*, and MOB for *mom of boys*. Mom laughs a fake, hollow laugh every time it comes up. She'll never go for it. MOB, on the other hand, has stuck. Not only that, it has extended to include Aunt Michelle's entire family. And the nickname is more fitting than I think she ever intended.

Seeing the MOB standing in the doorway, my chest felt tight, like all the air had been sucked out of it again. I should've guessed they would show up. At least once every summer, they overlapped our vacation, making the beach house seem cramped and small with so many people living under one roof. Dad and I had always planned most of our excursions for while they were in town.

Aunt Michelle was holding a suitcase, and Cisco and Diego were each wearing a backpack. It's a four-hour drive from their condo in Miami to here. They must've left home at the crack of dawn and obviously planned on staying for at least a few days.

"We're here for two whole weeks! Terrific, right?" Aunt Michelle announced as if reading my thoughts. "Angelo is tied up with work. He sends his best, but we were going nuts at home. *Right*, boys? Ugh, summer break. And there's nothing we need more than to be together *right* now . . ." She held my mom's gaze and said. "*Right*, sis?"

That was a lot of *right*s in one statement, but that was my aunt Michelle for you. She wasn't asking if anyone agreed with her. She was telling them they had to. She never allowed any room for opposition. Which was what worried me the most about her campaign to make us move.

My heart pounded in my ears. This was the last thing I needed. How could I prepare to persuade Mr. Shaw with the MOB around?

Mom pulled her face into a strained smile and nodded her head. "It's great to see you, Michelle. Thanks for driving all this way."

Everyone (minus me since I had one foot up the stairs already) launched into a round of hugs. The twins quickly dodged embraces and squirmed out of the circle. They made a break for it and Lanie took off after them, still covered in icing.

"Lanie," Grandma admonished. "Get back here! You're a mess."

Grandpa took Grandma's hand in his. "Oh, it'll clean. But this—her cousins being here—is good for her spirit."

Lanie adored Cisco and Diego. The twins turned three last month. When you added their ages together, they equaled Lanie in number of years lived, and exuded twice as much energy. The donut disaster apparently forgotten, my sister was all smiles and laughter as she disappeared into the living room.

Seeing what Grandpa said to be true, Grandma squeezed his hand in return and let Lanie go. Meanwhile, Aunt Michelle was cornering Mom. She splayed a hand across her chest and shook her head indignantly. It wasn't hard to imagine what she was saying. Aunt Michelle and Dad had never really gotten along. She had to be bursting with grievances against him that the divorce freed her to share.

That gnawed at me—I felt angry on his behalf. But watching her pin my mother down the way she was, it occurred to me that the MOB's sudden arrival might not be all bad. Aunt Michelle would keep Mom occupied, and the twins would keep Lanie out of my hair. Maybe they would forget all about my disappearance this morning, and I could focus on preparing to confront Mr. Shaw.

I quietly slipped away. Once I was alone in my room, I started thinking about the sea turtle again. How could I put together a project without access to my computer and a printer? Grandma and Grandpa weren't exactly technology junkies. But I needed facts. With the MOB here and everyone catching up, my chances of getting a ride to the library were nil, and my solo ride on the trolley hadn't exactly gone over well. What I really needed was Dad here. He'd know what to do about the loggerhead. He'd have more information, and he'd know how to help her.

I considered giving him a call, but there was still no way I could fake being happy over the phone. In person, on the other hand, I wouldn't have to pretend. If he were here, I would *be* happy.

Maybe he could come for visit. Maybe for my birthday? Then the summer wouldn't seem so terribly long. I almost didn't want to think about it, though. It was too much to hope for. Plus, my birthday was almost a week away. How many times would the turtle turn away again before then?

I shifted my thoughts to what I could do now. I had the photo I'd snapped on my phone at the aquarium. It wasn't impressive enough to persuade anyone—my conversation with Mr. Emerson had proved that. But I could make a poster with the facts it provided. It wouldn't be as attractive as color photos and informational graphs and charts, but maybe it would do the trick.

In a few short minutes, I'd raided Mom and Lanie's room for art supplies and was back in mine. I spread a large sheet of paper (poster board would have been better, but I had to work with what I had) and Lanie's colored pencils across the floor.

I was drawing a big green *L* for *loggerhead* at the top of the paper when Aunt Michelle knocked on my door. She entered without giving me a chance to welcome her in. Lanie's stuffed sloth was in one hand. Lanie's suitcase was in the other. I knew what she was going to say before she opened her mouth. "I'm bumping your sister out so I can bunk with your mom. Isn't that fun? Sisters must stick together. Right, Olivia? Friends come and go," she said, then murmured, "as do husbands, apparently . . . but sisters are forever."

I kept my mouth shut, but the look on my face must've said it for me.

"Or we can put the twins in here and Lanie and you can take the pullout couch downstairs, if that's what you'd prefer," she said in a not-so-friendly voice.

Generally, I like my aunt. She's fun and energetic. She wears bright colors, and when she talks, people listen. Her ideas are sometimes off-the-wall, but at least she's effective. At the moment, though, she wasn't my favorite person in the world.

When I finally stopped glowering and lowered my chin, she said, "I'll just drop these here, then," and dumped Lanie's stuff at the end of my bed.

Aunt Michelle paused and looked me over for a good long time. She examined the paper and colored pencils and the bright letter L. Her lips bunched to one side, and the skin around her eyes squinched together. I curled inwardly under her evaluation.

"How are you doing, Olivia?" she said, adding weight to each word.

My tongue felt like a rolled-up ball of cotton inside my

mouth. "Fine," I choked out. "I'm fine." My heart was heavy inside my chest, and I felt on edge about everything—Mom and Dad, her being here, and, at the moment, the turtle most of all.

Aunt Michelle smiled too sweetly and batted her lashes at me. "I'm glad to hear that," she said. She obviously didn't believe me.

My aunt wasn't gone five minutes when she came barging back in. By then, my piece of paper read, *LOGGER*.

"There's someone here to see you," my aunt said. "But don't take too long. Your sister and the twins want to watch a movie with you."

Someone was here to see me? Of course, I should've guessed who it would be, but it still surprised me to see Aiden standing on the front stoop.

"Hi," I said, hoping I didn't sound as anxious as I felt. I wanted to tell him everything and nothing all at once.

Aunt Michelle had followed me like a lost puppy and was practically breathing down my neck. I glanced over my shoulder and she held her ground. Apparently, she had no intention of giving Aiden and me any privacy. "Don't forget, Lanie and your cousins are waiting," she said in singsongy voice.

Aiden's eyes darted to her, then back to me. "Uh, my grandpa said you came by yesterday. I was hoping we could talk."

I bit my bottom lip while my aunt tapped her foot impatiently on the tile floor. "It's . . . not really a good time," I said, wishing I could make plans for later. The last thing I wanted, though, was for my aunt to know I was sneaking out at night.

Aiden's expression clouded. "Okay. I'll be around the *entire* day," he said, adding emphasis to *entire*. "In case you change your mind."

Catching his meaning, I nodded quickly and shut the door. He would be on the beach tonight.

"Come join us, Olivia," Aunt Michelle commanded. "I'm sure everyone is ready to start the movie now."

"Sure," I said. My footsteps into the family room were made heavy by both the brush-off I'd just given my friend and the thought of abandoning my turtle project. All I could do was keep my fingers crossed that I'd be able to sneak out and meet Aiden after dark.

The hard upper shell of a turtle is called a carapace.

The afternoon and evening dragged on and on with the movie, dinner, board games, and "family time." Lanie was close on my heels when the twins' eyelids finally got heavy and Aunt Michelle shooed everyone off to bed.

"Ah, my old room!" my sister said once we were upstairs. She then proceeded to make herself right at home.

"It was never *your* old room. It was *our* old room and now it's mine. You're just visiting." I knew I was being petty. It wasn't my room or Lanie's. The house belonged to Grandpa and Grandma, but I couldn't help myself. I was grumpy that the MOB had eaten up the entire day and I hadn't been able to talk with Aiden or work on my project.

Lanie carefully set the lettered olive on the nightstand,

scrunched up her face at my unfinished *LOGGER* paper, rolled it up, and spread out her own clean white sheet. She took over the colored pencils and the floor space by the bed and started working on a new list. Restraining an eye roll, I walked to the window and stared longingly at the beach.

Lanie dropped her pencil and coiled into a ready position. "Can we go down there?"

I stiffened. I had to choose my words carefully. I desperately wanted to meet Aiden and watch for the turtle again, but slipping out would be tricky with my sister around. When I couldn't think of anything better to say, I settled on redirection. "What's this list about?" I said, feigning interest.

"Oh!" Lanie repositioned herself on the rug. "I'm making a list of my favorite mystery creatures."

"I think you mean mythical creatures," I corrected.

"What?"

"Mythical creatures, not *mystery* creatures."

Her face darkened.

"It's all right, Lanie, just . . . go on."

She nodded, but instead of talking, she shoved her list at me to read.

1. Unicorn
2. Dragon

3. Fairy
4. Mermaid
5. Yeti

"These are great, Lanie. Really." Then I read the next few lines and wondered if "Mystery Creatures" was the right heading after all. "What's an elephat, though? Did you mean elephant? And what is this . . . porse?"

"An elephat is a cross between an elephant and a cat."

"I see. So a porse is a cross between a . . . pig and a horse?"

Lanie nodded her head enthusiastically.

"Okay." I smiled weakly. "Do you want me to help you come up with a few more?" I told myself I was just being nice to her so I wouldn't feel guilty when I ditched her later. But I must admit, after a while, I was having fun. "How about a bumble-lion—a cross between a bumblebee and a lion?"

"Can you imagine its sting?" Lanie's eyes went wide.

"Couldn't be any worse than getting eaten by a squidopus," I countered.

"What's that?" Lanie's eyes opened even wider.

"A cross between a giant squid and an octopus." Then a dark idea hit me. I'm not proud of it, but I was desperate to keep Lanie off the beach that night. If I had to keep track of her, I wouldn't be able to watch for the turtle.

"It's half octopus, right?" *Great, now I sounded like Aunt Michelle.*

I went on, "So it can crawl up on the beach for a few minutes, but only at *night*. It uses its, um, *nine* tentacles . . ." Thanks to Dad's Forrester Family Fabulous Facts, I knew an octopus had eight arms and a giant squid had eight arms, plus two feeding tentacles—ten in all. Nine tentacles sounded about right for a squidopus, but the thought of Dad sharing kernels of information nearly derailed me. My mouth went dry. But my desire to go down to the beach alone was overpowering. "Yeah. It, um, crawls to shore with its eight arms. Then it shoots its feeding tentacle out to find prey. The tentacle has these tiny sharp-toothed suckers that"—I grabbed her leg for effect—"stick in your skin as it wraps around you and drags you back into the ocean. Of course . . . Well, you probably don't want to know about that . . ." I said, peering at Lanie out of the corner of my eye to see if it was working.

"About what?" she asked, eyebrows springing up.

"Well, it's just that not everyone thinks they're mythical creatures. But, you know, only five percent of the ocean has been explored . . . People used to think giant squids were just a myth, too."

Lanie's lips parted in surprise. "You mean . . . ?"

"Yeah," I said gravely. "No one has captured a squidopus

on video *yet*, but there've been sightings. Not far from here, in fact."

I thought about laying it on even thicker—telling her how the feeding tentacle combs the beach for victims, then reels the prey toward its sharp beak and slices them into bite-size pieces—but Lanie looked sufficiently terrified already.

So as not to be too obvious, I threw out a few more "mystery creatures" before testing to see if the image of a squidopus had stuck with her. I came up with the dooster—a cross between a duck and rooster—and one she really liked—the slothird, which was basically a sloth with bird wings.

Then Lanie said, "How about a durtle? A cross between a dog and turtle—two of my favorite animals!"

I pursed my lips together. *Two of my favorites, also.* I couldn't take it any longer. I had to get outside. What if I'd missed seeing the turtle already? What if Aiden had come and gone?

After clearing my throat, I announced, "It's time to sleep." I went the extra mile of guiding her off the rug and tucking her into bed. I prayed she wouldn't say anything as I tiptoed toward the door.

"Where are you going?" she asked.

I straightened my shoulders and swung around to face her. "I'm turning off the light, then I'm going outside for a little while." Being honest with her, and gauging her reaction, was the only way I could be certain she wouldn't pretend to sleep and then sneak out after me.

"To the beach?" she asked.

"Yes."

I could see she was mulling it over. When she clutched her stuffed sloth and pulled it closer, I knew she was thinking about the squidopus.

"Be careful," she whispered, and ducked farther under the covers.

"Don't worry," I said, and quickly clicked off the lights. I didn't want her to catch a glimpse of the smile creeping onto my face. "I will."

As I snuck outside, I thought about Lanie. At six, she knew the difference between what was real and what wasn't, but the line was still blurry. In some ways, I envied her. I remembered what it was like to believe in magic and fairy tales and happily-ever-afters. Maybe it was worth believing in monsters under the bed and the bogeyman if you could still have unicorns, friendly dragons, charms, and enchantments.

Aiden was nowhere to be found, but there was another piece of sea glass waiting for me at my hideaway. As I approached the dunes, it winked at me in the moonlight. Thinking it strange that yet another one had appeared, I slipped the mermaid tear into my pocket.

It was a clear, beautiful night. The breeze smelled like sea-water, like an invitation from the ocean—*come closer, come let me lap around your ankles and lull you deeper.* The day's events had drained me. Mom's tears. Lanie spilling donuts across the Beachcomber's lawn. The MOB's arrival—I emptied all of it with a long, deep exhale.

I wondered where the turtle was—somewhere in the inky abyss beneath the moonlit waters or skimming the surface beyond where I could see. I'm not sure how long I stayed out there, watching for her. Long enough that the moon changed position in the sky and I knew Lanie would be fast asleep.

I heard the clicking and whirring of Aiden's cube before anything else. Sure enough, he had all the colors clicked into place by the time he plopped down in the sand beside me.

"I was worried you'd left already," I said. "Earlier, when you came to the house, I couldn't . . . my aunt . . . she . . . I didn't want to . . . my family . . . they . . ." Unable to complete a sentence, I gave up and ended with "I'm sorry."

For a while, Aiden didn't say anything. Then his bony shoulders rose upward in a shrug. "Why do you do that?"

"Do what?"

"Care so much about what everyone else thinks and does."

"I don't," I said, maybe a little too forcefully.

Aiden's eyebrows rose above his glasses. "Oh, so the reason

you wouldn't talk to me earlier wasn't because of your aunt? I guess you didn't want to talk to me, then." He pouted. "You haven't since you got here."

"That's not fair," I said. "I did . . . I *do* want to talk to you." Despite how badly I wanted to smooth things over with Aiden, we were off to another rocky start.

"Then maybe you should try doing more of what *you* want and less of what everyone expects from you."

I began to protest, then clamped my mouth shut. I'd spent the entire afternoon watching a kiddie movie with Lanie and the twins, then entertaining them while the adults talked. I'd wasted a good portion of the day trying to please my family instead of doing something really important to me—working on my project. How could I defend myself when Aiden was right? I changed the subject. "What did you want to talk about?" I asked hesitantly. What if he asked about my dad?

Aiden's chest heaved and collapsed as he inhaled deeply, then let the air out. "I don't know," he said at last. "I just needed to get out of Grandpa's place. He said you came by yesterday . . . so I thought . . . I don't know what I thought. He and Mom have a lot of things to discuss right now, so I decided to give them some space."

I wasn't sure if that made me feel better or worse. Maybe worse—he'd just been looking to get out of his grandpa's unit, not searching for me. And I wondered what his mom and Mr. Emerson had to discuss? When he didn't explain, I said, "I met Mr. Shaw today."

"Yeah?" Aiden dropped the cube he'd been holding. It fell to his lap. "Good for you."

"What's that supposed to mean?" I said, slightly hurt by the tone of his voice.

"Nothing," Aiden said. "He's just making things rough on Grandpa. That's all."

"How?"

"So, the old owner . . ." Aiden sat up straight, suddenly more animated than I'd seen him this trip. "He appreciated all Grandpa does for the Beachcomber. But Mr. Shaw wants to hire an outside company to manage the inn. He gets extra money if he can rent out Grandpa's place, too. But then Grandpa will be out of a job *and* a home." Aiden's voice grew higher as he continued talking. "Mom wants him to move in with us, but our apartment only has two bedrooms. I don't mind sharing, but Grandpa says I shouldn't have to bunk with an old man. Now he's working long hours, doing extra stuff around the inn. He wants to prove he's 'irreplaceable.'" Aiden tilted his body closer to mine. "He can't lose this job. He says no one else is going to hire a dinosaur like him."

Those might've been the most words I'd ever heard Aiden

string together in one sitting, and I wondered how long they'd been waiting to come out. I knew all about things that were hard to talk about. I wondered if Aiden had been acting more serious this summer because of what was going on with his grandfather. Maybe he wasn't too old and too cool to mess around with me now. Maybe he was just worried.

During his outpouring, he'd stared off into the distance. Now he peered from the corner of his eye, doing a bad job pretending he wasn't looking at me.

"That's terrible," I said. I sifted grains through my fingers, then pressed my palm into the sand. "I'm planning to talk to Mr. Shaw tomorrow . . ." I hedged. "Maybe I can tell him to speak with my grandparents. They could say good things—tell Mr. Shaw what a hard worker your grandpa is and how valuable he's been to the inn all these years. They've known him a long time."

Aiden turned his head to look at me straight on. "I don't know," he said skeptically. "I'm not sure Mr. Shaw is the type of person you can reason with."

That wasn't exactly what I wanted to hear. My shoulders must've drooped a little, because Aiden cocked his head and said, "Olivia? Why are you planning to talk to Mr. Shaw?"

Olivia, not *Liv*. Like most everyone else, he regularly switched between my name and nickname. This time, though, it sounded formal. Distant. Was it worry for his grandpa, or did he view me differently this summer? I still couldn't tell.

I was nervous to share my plan. I wouldn't be able to stand it if he told me my idea was dumb and childish. But then he lowered his chin and gazed up at me from beneath his dark lashes. He said, "Come on, Liv. I spilled the beans about my grandpa. Tell me what's going on with you. Please?"

He *had* opened up to me. That meant something. And his bad mood seemed to be evaporating. He seemed like he truly cared. I stared back into his dark, pleading eyes, and just like that, the wall between us evaporated. Everything came pouring out. *Everything.*

I told him about the divorce first. Once I got going, I wondered why I hadn't said something sooner. It felt so much better to unload. Aiden sat very still while I talked. I found his hand in the sand and rested my fingers on top of his.

Then I told him what I'd found out about bright lights and turtles at the aquarium, and the MOB trying to get Mom to move us here, and my plan to confront Mr. Shaw armed with facts. I was like an open balloon sputtering words instead of air.

As Aiden listened, he flipped his hand over and laced his fingers between mine.

When I finished, he was quiet. "Well?" I asked. "What do you think?"

"About which part?"

Honestly, it would've been nice to know his thoughts on all of it. "My project and Mr. Shaw," I said. Then, remembering how doubtful he'd been the first time I'd mentioned my suspicions about the light, I tacked on, "I have proof now."

Aiden seemed to be suppressing a grin. "Well, I don't think you'll be able to get him to *see the light*. Get it? See the light, like understand something he didn't before and, you know, see the light." He gestured toward the luminous inn.

I tipped my head toward the stars, smiling and groaning at the same time. This was the Aiden I'd been missing. The one who could make me laugh even when I was down.

"Terrible joke," he said, "but I couldn't resist."

We both seemed to notice at the same time that he was still holding my hand. He cleared his throat and let my fingers go. The moment was over, and he was solemn Aiden again. "Thank you for telling me about your dad. I'm really sorry." I nodded and he continued. "And I didn't mean to be so grumpy and act like I didn't believe you about the Beachcomber scaring the turtle away. The light from the inn is bad and Mr. Shaw should know about it. But please don't bring my grandpa into it. If he loses his job, I won't be coming here." He paused, then glumly added, "I probably wouldn't see you anymore."

The ache in my chest was so hard and sudden, I could

hardly breathe, let alone say anything. By then, I'd been on the beach for a while and had given up on the turtle making an appearance. It seemed nothing good would come that day. But this bombshell was the worst. It was the beginning of summer. We were supposed to be catching up, not saying goodbye. I couldn't bear *another* separation.

9

Florida is the world's most popular nesting site for loggerheads, with tens of thousands of nests built each year.

When I snuck back inside, I heard the murmur of voices coming from the kitchen. It didn't surprise me. Mom and Aunt Michelle had met downstairs in the middle of the night on other reunions, chatted until the wee hours of the morning, and slept until noon the next day. It had always driven Dad crazy.

Mom's voice was too soft to make out what she was saying, but the other voice carried. "Olivia disappeared on the trolley for over an hour," Aunt Michelle said. "You have to face the fact that she was running away. Obviously, her plan failed, and she didn't get very far. But you know it's just a matter of time before she tries again."

I stopped dead in my tracks. They were talking about me.

I hadn't been running away. I'd only gone to get a photo of the pier.

"You *need* to keep a closer eye on her," Aunt Michelle continued. "She's not adjusting well. You know how close she and her father were. And this strange boy showing up to speak with her? That's how it all starts, you know. Turn your back, and they get in trouble."

How close we *were*? Were, as in past tense? Anger flared inside me. What did she know? And Aiden wasn't a strange boy. He was Aiden. My friend, and the only person I'd really been able to talk to lately. I fisted my hands until my fingernails cut into the skin of my palms.

"Olivia is entering her teenage years . . . And you know her father is going to be preoccupied with work. What kind of supervision will she and Lanie receive while they're at his apartment? Think about it. You'll have more help here. Besides, the less the girls are around that man, the better. Olivia already acts too much like him. I heard her talking down to Cisco this afternoon. He said there was a lion in the video they were watching, and she just had to correct him." Aunt Michelle changed the pitch of her voice. "'It's not a lion, Cisco; it's a leopard.'"

I threw a hand over my mouth to smother a gasp. I'd sounded nothing like my aunt's imitation—all snooty and condescending. I'd only been trying to teach Cisco something, not make him feel bad.

"Can you imagine?" Aunt Michelle continued. "He's only three. You know better than anyone what it feels like to be belittled. Is that how Olivia treats her sister? Is that really the life you want for them?"

How could she say such awful things? And if anyone "belittled" Mom, it was her. I was about to burst in on them—tell my aunt she didn't know everything—when I heard a muffled sob. I flinched. Mom was crying again. Me charging in and giving Aunt Michelle a piece of my mind would only upset Mom more. Plus, I couldn't come unhinged without proving Aunt Michelle's point—that I wasn't adjusting well.

It wasn't easy, but I pulled back all my anger and hurt—contained it deep beneath my skin. There was an icy-hot burn in my chest, and I knew it was from repacking everything inside. I couldn't listen in anymore. If I did, I might explode.

I retreated to my room on the pads of my bare feet. I was careful not to make a peep, but my heart was banging so loudly when I slipped beneath the bedsheets, I was afraid it would wake Lanie. It was a very long time before I was calm enough to sleep.

When a ding from my phone woke me early the next morning, Lanie had already slipped out. Sleep had helped some. I felt drained, but at least the blood in my veins was no longer boiling.

For a minute, I relished the enormity of the bed without my sister crowding in beside me. Then I rolled over to retrieve my phone.

Your big day is coming, Olivia. Sweet 13! What's on your wish list? I want to make your birthday special.

I sat up straight in bed and carefully considered what to say. Dad's question seemed ripe with opportunity. I didn't want to blow it.

The thing was, I knew exactly what I wanted. I just couldn't find the nerve to come right out and ask for it. It took me close to five minutes to word my response, *I would like a grand gesture.*

I saw this movie once where a guy gave up his job and moved across the country to be with his girlfriend. She called it a "grand gesture" and broke into tears. I figured that was as close to saying what I wanted, without outright asking him to come visit.

Dad took almost as long to respond as I had. When he did, he said, *I don't suppose you'd settle for a pony?* He was trying to kid his way out, but I wasn't about to let him off the hook. *A grand gesture, please,* I typed again.

Okay. I'll see what I can come up with . . . BTW, I'm not

ashamed to admit I'm living my summer vicariously through you. So, what fun things do you have planned for today in the land of paradise?

What did I have planned? Completing my project and confronting Mr. Shaw. Although, I didn't think Dad would consider that fun.

The MOB is here, I texted back. He wouldn't think that was fun, either, but at least it was honest.

I take back what I said about paradise. Dad's response was swift. It made me chuckle, then wince. I had to admit, Dad's wit could be cutting.

Dropping my phone, I moved to the floor, unrolled my paper, and set to work. I felt bad for ignoring my family all morning. But then I remembered what Aiden said—that I shouldn't worry so much about pleasing everyone else.

Of course, he'd also said that Mr. Shaw wasn't the kind of person you could reason with. I sure hoped Aiden was wrong about *that*.

I poured myself into making the poster as eye-catching and informational as possible with my limited resources. Without a ruler, the lettering was a little slanted, and I'd squished some of the facts together on one side when I'd run out of room. But overall, I was proud of my work, and I was feeling good about my plan.

I was going directly to the person in power, with all the right information. Mr. Shaw would come around, and Mr. Emerson wouldn't have to be involved.

Before we parted the previous night, Aiden had told me Mr. Shaw lived in an enormous house in Sarasota, and that he usually left work early every day. It was after 2:00 p.m. by the time I was satisfied with my project. I'd skipped lunch and my stomach was growling, but I didn't want to miss Mr. Shaw and delay getting the problem taken care of.

Timing my exit for when Aunt Michelle was putting the twins down for a nap, I slipped out of the house unnoticed. I headed straight for the lobby of the Beachcomber. I hadn't been inside the inn very many times before. Aiden almost always came to me. But it was clear that as many renovations had been done on the inside as the out. Maybe more. There was new bamboo flooring and an area rug with fancy furniture sitting on top of it. The old décor had been a little bit of everything thrown together. This had a decidedly maritime feel with shell-shaped coffee tables and waving hints of blue all over the place. And the place was bustling. Suitcases were being wheeled in and out, and multiple guests were waiting at the counter.

Mr. Shaw was schmoozing a woman whose pasty skin gave her away as a new arrival. With my poster tucked carefully beneath my arm, I approached from behind and waited for a lull in the conversation to make my presence known.

"Can I just say, those are terrific shoes." Mr. Shaw complimented the woman on her coral-colored heels with neat little bows on the toes.

The skin on the tops of her feet bulged. The heels looked unbearably tight. They looked anything but "terrific" to me. But the woman lit up at his attention and squeezed his arm. "Well, aren't you the sweetest."

Mr. Shaw bowed slightly toward her and said, "Anything you need during your stay here, Ms. Fry, let the front desk know. We'll take good care of you." Then he swung around and nearly bumped straight into me.

"Mr. Shaw, I need to talk to you," I said before I could chicken out.

His face froze in a plastered-on smile. "What is it?"

What happened next was sort of a blur. I remember holding my poster out for him to see and barreling headfirst into my spiel. I'd memorized every last word on the page, and I rapidly repeated all of them. I spoke so swiftly that what I was saying was barely comprehensible. But it *was* comprehensible. By the time I got around to recounting what I'd seen on the beach—the loggerhead turning away—tears had sprung into my eyes. It was embarrassing, but I went on pleading my case.

The woman in the coral-colored heels flanked my side. "Oh, honey," she said. "That's just awful. Those poor turtles. Why, something must be done about this," she petitioned Mr. Shaw.

"Of course," Mr. Shaw said. His smile never wavered. "Would you please follow me to my office?" he said to me, and then to Ms. Fry, "I assure you, this young lady and I are going to put our heads together and find a satisfying solution to this unfortunate problem as quickly as possible."

"That's wonderful," Ms. Fry said. "I'm so relieved to hear you say that." Then she was happily on the move, dragging a wheeled suitcase behind her.

I felt relieved, too. Mr. Shaw spun around and motioned for me to follow. We went behind the welcome counter and entered a little room with a massive mahogany desk. When Mr. Shaw shut the door behind us, I expected him to either start making calls or brainstorming ideas to fix the lighting right away. Instead, he ripped the poster from my hands and tore it in half.

"I want you to leave," he said coolly. "You will not disturb my guests and ruin my business. I don't ever want to see you on Beachcomber property again. Is that clear?"

His sudden change in demeanor caught me off guard. I was speechless. He peeked out the office window, and after Ms. Fry had turned a corner and was out of sight, he practically shoved me back out the door we'd just walked in.

I had to keep moving to keep his hands off the small of my back. By the time I reached the lobby, I was in a light jog. I didn't stop running until I was back at the beach house.

For days after, the encounter with Mr. Shaw haunted me. My cheeks burned every time I thought about it. I knew I'd done nothing wrong, but the memory filled me with shame. Certain members of my family would be appalled if they heard I was causing trouble next door. And what would Aiden think? He'd tried to warn me about his grandpa's boss. Yet I'd been so gullible following Mr. Shaw into his office like that, thinking he would help. When he banished me, I'd been so stunned I hadn't even protested. I felt both wronged and at fault. I should've tried harder.

To make matters worse, Dad kept asking what I was up to. I needed more photos of our favorite spots around the island. My friends had been hounding me for updates, too. But every time I even thought about jumping on the trolley, the MOB got in the way. I almost made it out the front door once, when Diego yelled, "WHERE YOU GOING, COUSIN LIV?" at eardrum-rattling volume.

Aunt Michelle was on me in a heartbeat. "Where *are* you going, Olivia?" she asked in a disapproving tone. One that said I was going exactly nowhere.

At least her eyes and ears around the house—aka the

twins—went to bed early, and I was still able to sneak out after dark.

But even the beach didn't provide the solace it had before. The image of the turtle turning around and crawling back into the ocean was imprinted on my brain. Every night I didn't see her, I grew more anxious. I grew more desperate than ever for Dad to come.

Mr. Shaw would never be able to chase Dad away from the inn. Dad would stand his ground. Dad would know exactly how to make Mr. Shaw do something about the lighting. The thing was, I was afraid to ask Dad to visit for fear he'd say no. I wasn't sure my heart could handle another rejection. Over the past few days he'd taken stabs at what I meant by a grand gesture. So far, his guesses included: a photobook for the pictures I would take this summer, a GoPro, and photography lessons for my birthday.

Two days before I turned thirteen, I texted, *My birthday is almost here*, hoping against hope he'd say he was coming. *Did you figure out what to get me?*

Yes! I can't wait, he texted back, followed by a winking emoji.

That was strange. I'd expected him to apologize for not coming up with a grand gesture. I'd expected him to say my gift was in the mail. There was no way he'd figured it out, was there?

Is it something that comes in a box? I texted back.

Nope.

Is it on its way? It wasn't like Dad to pay ridiculous prices to mail something. If it was a package, he would've sent it already.

Not yet.

When will it arrive?

No more questions, Liv. You'll ruin the surprise!

Please? Give me one hint.

Okay. Let's just say, I thought seeing a familiar face or two on your birthday would really brighten your day.

Did that mean he was coming? But he said a familiar face or two . . . Who else would he bring? Maybe one of his friends from the university? Probably Dr. Nguyen. The two of them had gone to academic conferences together before, and I wouldn't blame Dad for not wanting to travel alone. It didn't matter, as long as he came.

I really want to see YOUR face, I texted back.

Don't worry. You will.

I sprang from the bed, nearly knocking my phone to the floor, and punched the air with my fist. "Yes!" Dad was coming. In a couple of short days, we'd be together again. In just a few short days, I'd have my biggest ally here with me on the island. Finally! Some good news for me *and* the turtle.

10

**Female loggerhead turtles build between
one and seven nests per year.**

Not knowing how to help the sea turtle had been hanging over me like a dark cloud, but on my birthday, it felt like the sun was breaking through. It didn't bother me that Lanie's arm was draped across my shoulder and that she was mouth breathing right in my face. I nudged her arm off me and gently rolled her away. She curled up and snuggled under the coverlet, looking all small and sweet.

I shook my head, mystified that I could be in that good a mood—that my sister seemed adorable instead of annoying. But there it was. I knew when Dad came, he could talk to Mr. Shaw. Dad was smart. He would get the problem sorted out. So, nothing could bring me down.

I estimated his travel time in my head. It was a

three-and-a-half-hour flight from Denver to Tampa. Then there was the drive down and over the Sunshine Skyway Bridge, which added another hour. It would most likely be early afternoon before he'd arrive. Surely, he'd be in time for dinner. Last summer, we'd talked about celebrating my thirteenth birthday with a fancy dinner on the beach at the Sandbar.

The bubbling excitement was almost more than I could bear. It was like waking up at 2:00 a.m. on Christmas morning and knowing the wait would kill you.

Of all people, Aunt Michelle was the one who saved me from myself. Her knock on the bedroom door woke Lanie, and my sister drew to a seated position on the bed beside me. "Happy birthday, Liv," she said blearily.

"Thanks." I smiled at Lanie—something I hadn't done for a while—and her face broke into a grin.

"Girls, hurry down to breakfast!" Aunt Michelle called from the other side of the door. "Grandpa cooked a special meal to kick off Olivia's fourteenth trip around the sun. We're all eating together. Fun, right?"

At home, if Lanie and I ate breakfast at the same time, that was *something*. And it was usually a slice of peanut butter toast in the car on the way to school.

Next thing I knew, I was staring at the back side of my sister's head as she bounded out of the room. She was more excited for my birthday breakfast than I was. Well, maybe . . . It warmed my heart knowing Grandpa had gone to all that effort.

By the time I got dressed and made my way to the dining room, Aunt Michelle had dragged everyone to breakfast. Grandma had set the dining room table with her finest china and Grandpa had gone all out. He carried in plates garnished with fresh fruit from the market and poached eggs with avocados on toasted rye bread.

Lanie was seated at the table, sandwiched between the twins. When Grandpa set a plate in front of her, she took one look at the green stuff mashed between her eggs and toast and turned a little green herself.

"Um, can I have cereal?" she pleaded while batting her eyelashes.

At the same time, Cisco reached across her to swipe a piece of cantaloupe from his brother's plate. He toppled the carafe of orange juice in the center of the table. It ran off the edge and onto my shorts, and I pulled my phone from my pocket and set it on a dry spot on the tablecloth.

Across from me, Grandma and Aunt Michelle sprang into action. Grandma ran for towels and Aunt Michelle dabbed at the mess with her napkin.

While Aunt Michelle was distracted, Diego disappeared beneath the table. He reemerged holding Cisco's left shoe.

Cisco happily took the bait. He leaped from his chair and chased Diego in circles around the table, trying to retrieve it. Diego taunted and held the shoe just out of reach. Mom bit her lip and Lanie giggled, enjoying the show.

I righted the empty carafe, and Aunt Michelle turned her attention toward me. For once, instead of scrutinizing, she smiled apologetically.

Grandma returned, breathing through her nose, no doubt to stay calm. Her jaw was clenched as she mopped up the OJ. Grandpa mumbled to himself while he rushed around picking up dishes and soggy toast, attempting to salvage breakfast.

By the time order was restored and Cisco and Diego had been wrangled back into their seats, everyone was staring at me. Even the twins.

"What do you have to say for ruining Cousin Olivia's birthday breakfast?" Aunt Michelle said pointedly.

"We're sorry," the twins dutifully replied in unison.

"It's all right, really," I said. And it was. Nothing could've put a damper on my mood just then—not with Dad's grand gesture right around the corner. I felt the worst for Grandpa.

Lanie begged for cereal a second time, and the twins chimed in, "Us too, us too!"

As Aunt Michelle led the herd into the kitchen, Grandpa sighed and said, "If everyone is having cereal, we're going to need more milk." I felt so bad that all his hard work had been turned into a soggy orange-juicy mess.

"I'll go with you," I offered. There was plenty of time before Dad would make an appearance. I needed as many distractions as possible.

We took the trolley to the corner store for a gallon of milk. We were in and out of the store and back to the beach house in no time.

"Liv!" my sister sprang on me as soon as we returned. "Your phone *never* stopped dinging while you were gone. Here!" It wasn't until she shoved my phone into my hands that I remembered leaving it on the dining room table.

There was a lot of chaos in the moments that followed. The adults and Lanie gathered around me curiously, and I attempted to melt into the marble-tile floor. My phone went off a second after she handed it to me, and Lanie let out a triumphant "See!"

When it dinged again, my own curiosity got the better of me. I had to check. My phone had been flooded with video messages. There was one from Mia, and Abigail, and Josephina and Riley and Talisha and more.

Every time I opened a message, one of my friends' faces would pop on the screen. There was Mia singing "Happy Birthday" as her new puppy chewed a squeaky toy in the background.

Josephina shaking pompons and saying "Hooray, Olivia! Happy sweet thirteenth!" Each one was a personalized birthday message and the last one was from Dad.

My heartbeat thundered in my ears as I bolted for the stairs. Once I was shut in my room, I scrolled to the bottom and opened the message from Dad.

"Hi, sweetheart! Did you know Jacques Cousteau was also born on June eleventh? Of course you did." My on-screen father shook his head. "I remind you of it every year, don't I? Well, I hope you enjoy seeing all the familiar faces today. The pictures you've been sending of the island have helped a great deal." Dad choked up, and I felt my own larynx grow tight, like someone was slowly strangling me. He cleared his throat and forced a smile back on his face. "Um, I thought you might be wanting the same in return—to see what's going on here. Your friends were so great and excited to participate. I think they miss you almost as much as I do. Okay, well, give me a call when you get this. I love you, Liv! Happy birthday." Then his video was over.

It hit me with heartbreaking certainty. This was Dad's grand gesture. Enlisting my friends to send birthday wishes was his "big surprise." He wasn't coming to Anna Maria Island. He wasn't going to talk to Mr. Shaw. The realization was disorienting. The hurt was sharp and deep. I staggered to my bed and collapsed, feeling incredibly stupid for ever thinking he would come.

11

Loggerhead sea turtles lay from one hundred to two hundred eggs in a single nest.

I didn't call Dad. I didn't respond to any of the messages from my friends. I turned off my phone, tossed it in my nightstand, and slammed the drawer shut.

I was devastated—for me and the turtle.

When Mom knocked on my door shortly after I'd fled the kitchen, it was all I could do to muffle the sound of my tears. "Your dad's on the phone . . ." she said. She paused, waiting for an answer I couldn't give—my throat was too raw, the emotion rising in my chest too strong. "He called *my* cell . . . Said you aren't answering yours . . . He'd like to wish you a happy birthday, Liv." Her voice was so low, I could barely hear her through the door.

While trying to compose myself enough to speak, a gurgle escaped my lips.

"What was that, honey?"

"Tell him I'm not feeling well," I said. And I wasn't. My stomach was roiling, my palms were sweaty, and my body felt weighted down with disappointment.

It took most of the morning for me to pull myself enough together to rejoin my family downstairs. When I did, Grandma commented on my pale skin, and Grandpa insisted on boiling some fresh ginger tea. Mom laid a hand on my forehead. Aunt Michelle narrowed her eyes suspiciously. The twins and Lanie were too busy playing to pay me any attention at all.

I stretched my lips into a smile. "I feel better," I said, even though my heart felt cleaved in two. I acted excited when they presented me with gifts, even though I hadn't felt so low since Mom and Dad announced their divorce.

Grandma and Grandpa gave me a skin-care kit. I knew exactly which one of them had picked it out. Lanie and Mom gave me an art supply set they'd ordered online. I'd seen Lanie drooling over the thumbnail photo of it weeks ago. Again, I knew exactly who'd picked it out. Aunt Michelle gave me a new swimsuit cover-up that looked almost identical to one of hers.

It's not that I was ungrateful for their gifts, but Dad's was the most thoughtful. I would've liked it—I missed him and my friends, and seeing their faces would've cheered me up—if I hadn't been expecting something more.

I was so blue, I almost didn't visit the beach that night. But, of course, I had to. I couldn't give up on the sea turtle just because Dad wouldn't be able to help her. I had to find another way.

Aiden was waiting at my dune. He sprang to his feet when he saw me. His eyes were bright behind his glasses. "Hey! Happy birthday! Know what else today is? That's right, my favorite holiday—National Corn on the Cob Day."

I smiled despite myself. Three years ago, Dad told Aiden I share a birthday with Jacques Cousteau. The following year, Aiden presented me with an ear of corn on my birthday and told me how pleased he'd been to discover he could celebrate me and his favorite vegetable on the same day. He brought me an ear of corn last June 11, too.

I tried not to notice his hands were empty this year. It was sweet of him to remember my birthday, and I didn't feel up to eating corn anyway. It didn't matter that he hadn't brought me any this year. It didn't. But my smile faded anyway.

"What's wrong, Liv?" he asked.

I sat down in the sand and he lowered himself beside me.

"Is this because . . . I mean, did you go to Mr. Shaw?"

I shrugged, then nodded my head. I told Aiden about how Mr. Shaw had tricked me into thinking he was on my side, how he'd turned on me, ripped up my project, and chased me out of the Beachcomber. I felt stupid enough recounting that story. I couldn't bear to reveal that I'd also foolishly been convinced Dad would come and fix everything, but now I was back to square one.

Even though I was keeping the most embarrassing part to myself, Aiden seemed to be growing more and more uncomfortable as I spoke. He squirmed. He turned his Rubik's Cube over in his hands, examining it from every angle.

"Hmm," he said when I'd finished.

"'Hmm'? That's all you have to say?" I may have droned my way through it, but I'd expected a stronger reaction from him. I wanted him to be indignant on my behalf.

"What do you want me to say?" His voice sounded low and sad, with a twinge of something else. Was he annoyed with me?

"Oh, I don't know. Maybe that you'll help?" I said tersely. "Maybe that you'll knock some sense into your grandfather. He'll listen to you." Even as I was saying it, I knew it was a lost cause. Aiden was turning his head away from me. The moon was shining bright enough tonight that I could see the pink tingeing his cheeks. "I can't do that, Liv. I told you how much pressure Grandpa's under. Going against Mr. Shaw will get him fired for sure."

I didn't want Mr. Emerson to be fired, but I didn't want the turtle to be scared either. I probably should have explained, but instead I shut down and crossed my arms. He crossed his, too, and just like that, a wall was up between us again.

I blinked backed tears and my heart seized inside my chest. I'd thought our friendship was back on track, heading toward normal. But I'd been wrong.

Aiden and I both lived separate lives from the ones we lived here. Mine in Colorado, and his where he lived on the mainland with his mom. He had plenty of friends from school who lived near his apartment complex. He could hang out with them most of the summer. But when he was visiting his grandfather, I was his only option. It wasn't like he would choose to hang out with me if any of his other friends were on Anna Maria Island. But I *would* choose him, and knowing that made things extra hard.

"You're outgrowing me," I choked out while staring at a few coarse grains of sand mixed in with all the fine.

"What? No," Aiden said.

"You act nice when you're around me because you don't want to hurt my feelings, but it's not like you enjoy hanging out with me anymore. You're just killing time. You think I'm childish and that the turtles and the light don't really matter. It's fine," I said. "You don't have to ask your grandfather for help. And you don't have to come see me ever again." It wasn't fine, but I didn't want him to know how much I cared about him. And if he didn't feel the same way about me, it was better if he didn't come around at all. It would hurt too much.

"That's not true," he protested.

I wanted to believe him, but I was sick of being disappointed. "Just leave me alone," I said.

Aiden nodded his head, drew himself to a standing position, and brushed the sand from his shorts. Before leaving, he said, "Happy birthday, Olivia." He paused, then added, "Here, I found this in the sand." When I reached out, he pressed an object into my hand, then made a straight line for the Beachcomber.

It was another piece of sea glass. Aiden had gotten to it before I arrived. I palmed the mermaid tear and stroked it like a worry stone. It didn't soothe. Nothing did.

When a dark shadow glided across the swath of moonlit water a short while later, my heart didn't leap in my chest. When the sea turtle clumsily crawled out of the ocean, I didn't feel happy. Not like the first time I'd seen her. It was as if my heart knew what was coming and refused to celebrate.

"Please," I whispered feebly. "It's safe here. Come ashore.

Come home." I silently willed the turtle to crawl across the sand. I thought again how loggerhead turtles return to the beach where they were born to lay their eggs. She belonged here more than we did.

The turtle didn't make it as far as last time before turning back. Why would she continue with all that light glaring in her eyes? As I watched her go, my blood grew hotter and hotter until it boiled.

Without giving it a second thought, I sprang to my feet and stormed toward the *incandescent* Beachcomber. I took a different path than Aiden had. He'd turned and walked toward his grandfather's unit at the front of the building. I walked along the beach, then crossed the dunes, went through the gate, and arrived at the edge of the pool. It was empty.

"It's so important to keep these lights on, even when *no one* is swimming?" I fumed. Then I hurled the piece of sea glass with all my might. Dad always said I had a good arm. The glass shattered, and the bright light beside the pool went dark. When it did, the blood pulsed harder in my veins—not with fear or anger, but with a feeling of justice. It felt good. It felt gratifying.

That was until I turned toward Grandma and Grandpa's beach house and saw Lanie watching me out the window.

Her face was plastered to the pane of glass, her jaw slack with disbelief.

When my sister saw me looking, she took a step back and was engulfed by the darkness. When I crept into our bed, not five minutes later, she was silent. I knew she was only pretending to sleep.

12

The cavity a loggerhead turtle digs for a nest is eighteen to twenty-two inches in depth.

Lanie was normally a noisy and active sleeper. Her feet would find their way to the backs of my knees. Her elbows would catch me in the ribs. She'd mutter stuff I usually couldn't understand. After I made up that bit about the squido-pus, it got even worse. She squirmed and whimpered in her sleep, and one night I caught her swatting at her own arms and moaning, "No, no, too many tentacles."

When that happened, I did my best to comfort her. I even tucked her stuffed sloth under her arm, but the nightmares continued, making me feel about the size of plankton.

The night I broke the light, however, it was me doing all the tossing and turning. Lanie never could keep a secret. It was only a matter of time before she tattled. I had to get ahead of the storm.

During my nighttime restlessness, I decided to do two things. One, confess to breaking the light, and two, try to enlist my grandparents to help with the turtle and the Beachcomber. Grandpa had a peacekeeper's heart, though. I wasn't sure he'd be that effective. Grandma was fiery enough, but I didn't know which way she'd fall. She might take Mr. Shaw's side after she learned about the broken light. Either way, I was running out of options.

I expected Grandpa, but it was Grandma I found in the kitchen first thing the next morning. She was making a packet of instant oatmeal. "You know the turtles . . ." I started.

"What, dear?" she asked.

Just as I opened my mouth to repeat myself, Grandpa entered behind me. *Good*, I thought, *now I can explain myself to both my grandparents before Lanie has a chance to rat me out.* "The turtles."

"Yes?" Grandma said, but a bewildered expression was blooming on Grandpa's face, which drew her attention away from me. It was then that I noticed the piece of paper in his hands. She took a step toward him. Then Aunt Michelle, the twins, and Mom appeared out of nowhere, and I was forgotten in the crowd.

Grandpa's voice was incredulous, and a hair louder than normal, when he spoke. "Mr. Emerson left a note on our door. He thinks one of the kids threw a rock at the Beachcomber and broke the security light by the pool."

A tiny gasp escaped my throat, then my airways shut down. So much for getting ahead of the storm. It was right on top of me.

Time seemed to stand still as my family digested the news. Then, in perfect synchrony, Grandma, Grandpa, Mom, and Aunt Michelle turned their attention not to me but to Cisco and Diego.

"It couldn't have been . . . I didn't turn my back on them for a second yesterday," Aunt Michelle said. "I'll talk to Mr. Emerson—tell him he's mistaken."

Grandma squeezed her hand. "You do that," she said.

I released my breath, thinking the storm may have swept on by when Lanie's voice rang out loud and clear with accusation. "It was Liv!" I turned and there she was, standing in the doorway, wiping sleep from her eyes with one hand and pointing at me with the other. "I saw her do it."

My family's necks turned to rubber and their heads whipped toward me.

When I didn't deny it, Aunt Michelle reeled on Mom and threw her hands in the air. "What did I tell you? She's turned into a delinquent."

This was not going the way I'd planned, but what had lately?

Mom shut down, of course, and let my aunt do all the talking. "You know, kids act out when their parents split. It's only natural, but you have to let them know it's not acceptable," the MOB declared.

Grandma fretted to herself loud enough that everyone could hear, and Grandpa tried to placate Aunt Michelle. "Now, now, now . . . I'm sure there's a reasonable explanation."

Nobody even asked me if I did it. *Why* I did it. Even if they had, my airways were still blocked. The words were stuck inside me.

Aunt Michelle ignored Grandpa and continued to bore down on Mom. "*Someone* needs to be a parent here. If you're not going to, then I will. I'm taking Olivia next door. She needs to apologize. She needs to take responsibility for her actions."

For a second, I thought Mom might hold her ground. I should've known better. The rise in her chest lasted only a second before she cowered and looked away.

"Olivia," Aunt Michelle bellowed. "Come with me."

Grandpa searched my face once more. I think if I'd said I didn't do it, he would've stepped in. He would've kept Aunt Michelle from dragging me next door. But I *did* do it. And it must've shown in my expression. Grandpa sighed and shook his head sadly.

"Olivia!" Aunt Michelle prodded.

I nodded my head and fell into step behind her.

· · ·

Something changed in me on the march next door. My heart, which had been beating rapidly, settled to an even thump-thump. My legs, which had felt like Jell-O, fell into a sure and steady stride. I was past caring what Aunt Michelle thought. I focused on what I had to do.

Aunt Michelle marched into the front lobby and jabbed the call bell with her pointy, watermelon-colored fingernail. She didn't say it, but I knew what she was thinking—that she was doing the right thing. That this was for my own good.

I was surprised when Mr. Shaw emerged instead of Aiden's grandfather. It seemed awfully early for him to be around. When he saw Aunt Michelle, his eyebrows rose with interest and his smile flowed smooth and oily. The instant he noticed me standing next to the MOB, though, his expression froze.

I jutted my chin as Aunt Michelle cleared her throat. "Hi, you're the new owner, right? We're staying next door and we got Mr. Emerson's note. About the light?"

For once, I was relieved my aunt never lets anyone else get a word in. She missed the bewilderment, followed by annoyance crossing Mr. Shaw's face. Mr. Emerson must've left my grandparents the note without saying anything to Mr. Shaw. Before he could question any of it, the MOB said, "My niece has something she needs to tell you. *Right*, Olivia?" I felt Aunt Michelle's hand press into the small of my back. She pressed even harder when she caught me glowering.

After that, I didn't hesitate. "I broke your pool light, Mr. Shaw. But I'm *not* sorry."

Mr. Shaw's eyes flashed with outrage, but after glancing at a guest standing at the coffee station, he held his smile.

Aunt Michelle gasped. "Olivia!"

I ignored her, and my words spilled out in one frenzied stream. "The turtle tried to come to shore again," I said. "All that light made her turn away. You're the one who should be apologizing!"

Mr. Shaw clenched his smiling teeth as I spoke, but remained silent.

Aunt Michelle's hand traveled from my back and clamped around my arm. Her fingernails dug into my skin. "What are you talking about?" she hissed in my ear. Then to Mr. Shaw, she said, "You'll have to excuse my niece. She's going through a difficult time."

Mr. Shaw's thin lips twitched but ultimately held their

upward curl. "Totally understandable. It's a volatile age," he said, gesturing toward me, then speaking to my aunt as if I weren't even there. "Such grit and passion, though, you almost have to admire it." He chuckled. "However, she's obviously mistaken. Misdirected anger perhaps—you said she's going through a difficult time?"

"Parents are divorcing. And the anger—that's what I've been trying to tell her mother," Aunt Michelle said. "She—"

"Stop it!" I screamed over my aunt. I couldn't take it anymore. Neither of them cared one bit about the turtle, and Mr. Shaw was laying on the charm again. But I knew better this time. I knew what he was really like. "Stop pretending, you . . . !" I lunged toward him. "You jerk!"

Aunt Michelle yanked me back. At the same time a cup clattered to the floor behind us. The guest at the coffee station scrambled to pick up shards of his mug, and Mr. Shaw's smile finally faltered.

He straightened his tie. "I think you'd better go," he said frostily. Then he bustled over to assist the guest with cleanup.

I resisted, but Aunt Michelle proceeded to drag me outside. Once we'd exited the building, she snatched my other arm. Locked in an embrace, she looked me in the eye. "I don't know what that was about, but it was entirely inappropriate.

What you did is called vandalism and it's a crime," she said. "I thought we might be able to smooth things over if you confessed, but now you'll be lucky if he doesn't call the police."

I steeled myself and tried to glare back at her, but my lip betrayed me with a quiver. Why did everything have to be so difficult? It'd felt good to break the light, but I didn't want to be in trouble with the law. I couldn't imagine trying to explain myself to a police officer—when I couldn't seem to even manage it with family.

Pinned beneath my aunt's scowl, I started to tremble. All my bravado drained away, and I felt small and alone again.

"Come on," she said, obviously exasperated. "This is something your *mother* will have to deal with now." She let go of my fist, but her other hand stayed wrapped around my forearm. She didn't let go until we were back inside the beach house.

As soon as I could, I wriggled out of her grasp and darted down the hallway, up the stairs. I didn't stop running until I'd thrown my bedroom door shut behind me. Aunt Michelle's voice carried through all three levels. Her words were muffled but decidedly angry.

I could only imagine what she was telling Mom about

me. But I didn't regret it. I didn't regret any of it. Not smashing the light to bits or telling Mr. Shaw that I wasn't sorry. Even if the police came, I wasn't sorry.

The squabble downstairs carried on for what seemed like hours. The clock on my dresser said seven minutes. For seven minutes, I mostly heard the buzz of Aunt Michelle's voice, but I could pick out others—Mom's, Grandma's, Grandpa's, even the twins whining about something. And then the front door slammed, and everything got quiet.

13

Female loggerhead sea turtles are twenty to thirty years old when they build nests for the first time.

The police never came, but Lanie did. She creaked the door open and peeked her head in. With her chin hung down she said in a small, remorseful voice, "The MOB went back to Miami." Then she set up camp on our bedroom floor and began whispering wishes into her shell.

My stomach was tied in knots. I couldn't believe I'd exploded like that. "Tell me what Aunt Michelle said before they left."

Lanie shrugged.

"Can you tell me why they left?"

"You."

I sighed. *That* I knew already. "Okaaay," I said slowly. What

I most wanted to know was if Mom was disappointed with me. If she'd been upset by my behavior. "What did Mom say?"

Lanie shrugged again.

I felt a sudden flicker of anger. "Could you be any less helpful?" I clipped.

Lanie shoved the lettered olive into her pocket and gathered her sloth and other belongings. "I'm moving back to Mom's room," she said, then stood there a minute, like she was waiting for me to stop her.

"Good," I said. "Great, actually."

She didn't move.

"Go already!"

Lanie huffed and stormed out of my room.

I tried to convince myself that I didn't care what had been said about me, that I didn't care what anyone said about me. But I did.

A few minutes later, Mom knocked on my door before entering. As she walked into the room, I kept my chin down and tried not to notice the deep lines around her eyes that meant she'd lost weight the last few weeks. She looked skinny in an unhealthy sort of way. Her face seemed even more hollow than it had that morning. She sat at the foot of my bed. She fidgeted and fiddled nervously with a bracelet on her wrist.

She was dealing with a heavy load right now, and I felt

terrible for making things worse. No matter how hard I tried to keep her happy, I kept failing at it.

When she finally spoke, she said, "I don't want you to blame yourself that Aunt Michelle left. I asked her to go because I'm trying to take control over my life. With her here, that wasn't possible."

Practically everything Mom said lately sounded rehearsed. She seemed like a walking, talking wax figure. All I wanted was for her to be real with me, but I didn't know how to tell her that without upsetting her more.

"I don't expect you to understand, Olivia, but it's something I need to do for myself," she continued stiffly. "Prove I'm capable of making my own decisions and living my life as I see fit. I don't agree with the way Aunt Michelle handled the incident this morning, but she was right about one thing. You shouldn't have thrown a rock at the inn."

I looked up and Mom held my gaze, as if she expected an explanation. I'd managed to bottle up my emotions tight and neat again, though. A leak wouldn't be good for either of us.

"I think I have a pretty good idea why you did it," Mom said. "Something happened with your dad yesterday, and you were upset, right? I know you and your father made plans last summer to celebrate your thirteenth birthday at the Sandbar.

I thought about making a reservation, but I knew it wouldn't be the same without your father there."

I nodded my head.

"So you were angry, and you took it out on the light next door. I get it."

I shrugged, since she was partially right.

"You understand that there has to be a consequence, don't you?"

I said nothing. There were so many things I should've said. Maybe I could've told Mom how I was feeling and the real reason I'd broken the light if she went back to the way she was before. Back when she babbled to herself and hummed tunes while flipping through the mail. Back when she doodled on grocery receipts and cursed at the TV when she thought no one was listening. That Mom, I could've talked to. If I said anything to her now, she'd only wind up crying in the pantry again.

"Okay, Olivia." Mom straightened her back. "Hand over your phone."

I never took my eyes off hers as I slid open the nightstand drawer. She glanced curiously at my pile of sea glass but said nothing about it. I retrieved my phone and placed it in her open palm.

Mom stared at the phone as though it were a foreign object. As much as she said she wanted control over her life, she *was* following a script. Like taking my phone was something she was supposed to do. As if the punishment made her a "good parent" or something. *Come on, Mom*, I thought. *Stop pretending.*

Now that she had it, she didn't seem to know what to do with it. Dad would've known. He would've explained how I could earn the phone back. Better yet, he would've come up with a more fitting punishment. I mean, how was me not having my phone supposed to fix the light?

Mom stood up awkwardly and swatted at her lap as if brushing away nonexistent crumbs. "I guess I'll put this in a safe place."

I felt sorry for her. As hard as she was trying to be strong, she was anything but. She was uncertain, brittle, and weak. It was . . . sad.

Right then and there, I ran out of pity. I was sick and tired of worrying that every little thing I did would unhinge her. I was sick and tired of disappointing everyone and being disappointed by them. What was the point in trying?

I couldn't take it anymore. My sympathy flared into frustration. Why did I have to keep it together so Mom could figure out her life? She was the adult, not me. I should've been able to talk to her without worrying she'd dissolve into tears.

All the anger and unhappiness I'd been trying to quell

gathered in the pit of my stomach. In that moment, every ounce of pain and fury and heartache I'd been feeling was directed at her. It was the same rage I'd felt when confronting Mr. Shaw, but this time instead of lunging, I inhaled sharply through my nose and glared. With my stony silence, I pushed her right out of my room.

14

Loggerhead sea turtles build their nests
primarily at night.

Other people would only let me down. That was the con-
clusion I drew from all of this. Dad, Aiden, Mom—they'd
all failed me in different ways. But it wasn't like I was
any better. I'd failed my family. I'd caused a commotion when
I'd taken off on the trolley and then a bigger mess by vandalizing Beachcomber property. I couldn't depend on my family,
but they couldn't depend on me, either. It was best for everyone
if I kept to myself.

I would avoid them all and remain in my room as much as
possible. But I could never give up the beach.

When the MOB had been around, Mom mostly stayed put
in the same room as Aunt Michelle after dark. But with Lanie

sleeping in Mom's room again, she took to roaming the house that night.

I could sense her restlessness through the walls. The rhythm of her footsteps on the landing outside my room was more wandering than purposeful. She was pacing. Sleepless in part because of me, no doubt.

The one time it grew quiet, and I thought she'd finally retreated to her and Lanie's room, I peeked out my door only to find the light on at the bottom of the stairs. Eventually, I fell asleep waiting for her to go to bed.

As soon as I woke the next morning, I crept outside. There was nothing but a growing crack of sunlight along the bottom edge of the darkened sky. I went directly to my secret place between the dunes and collected yet another mermaid tear. I briefly marveled at where all the pieces of sea glass were coming from. Then I wandered farther down the beach, until I was facing the Beachcomber. By then, the sun had risen enough to peek over the inn in a rounded glow instead of a thin orange line.

A woman sat drinking coffee on a balcony outside one of the rooms. She smiled and seemed totally unaware of the duress her accommodations were causing the turtle. I wondered if she would've been less friendly if she'd known I was responsible for shattering the pool light.

I also wondered where Aiden was and when he'd visit again—*if* he'd visit again. When I remembered telling him to just leave me alone, my heart felt tender in the way a bruise does when you run your finger across it.

I spun away from the inn and faced the ocean. That's when I saw the tracks and pushed everything else from my mind.

They'd been partially erased by early-morning beachgoers, but they were there if you knew what to look for. Trying not to get my hopes up, I followed the turtle treads to a place beyond the next dune where the sand looked sifted, swirled, and slightly indented. I knew instantly what I was looking at, and my heart thrummed happily inside my chest. She'd made it! The sea turtle had finally come all the way ashore. She'd made a nest.

She'd made a nest, but she'd made it . . . *here*.

The spot was far from ideal. It was near the gate in the picket fence surrounding the inn's pool. It was too close to the trail the guests took to the ocean. Then there were the chairs and umbrellas occasionally left strewn across the sand. When the eggs hatched, the baby turtles would need a clear path to the water. And what about the other lights on the Beachcomber Inn—the ones I hadn't smashed.

Panic wrapped its pincers around my heart. I'd wanted so badly for the mama turtle to come ashore, I hadn't fully considered what it would mean for her babies. This was not a safe place for them to be born.

My feet were running before I'd thought anything through. I pounded on Mr. Emerson's door seconds later. "Come on, open up," I said to myself as I fidgeted on his front porch.

When he didn't answer, I scurried to the front of the inn and inside the lobby. Mr. Emerson was checking in guests at the counter. His eyes flicked in my direction. A pained expression darted across his face before he returned his attention to the couple standing in front of him.

I bounced on my toes behind the guests for as long as I could stand it. They seemed like a nice-enough couple—young, with starry eyes for each other. Probably honeymooners or something. Ick.

"Excuse me," I said, and carved my way between the lovebirds and up to the counter. "I need to talk to you, Mr. Emerson."

"It's not a good time, Olivia," he said.

"But there's a nest on the beach!" As I blurted this out, I caught the guests exchanging a look behind my back—half-puzzled, half-annoyed.

Mr. Emerson came from behind the counter and pulled me aside. "I'm happy to hear that, but I can't be involved. I'm already in hot water for not going directly to Mr. Shaw about the broken light. I . . . I'm sorry."

Before I could explain how the nest was in a terrible location and that he *had* to get involved, the young woman pushed her way back in front of me. "We caught a red-eye flight to get here. We're exhausted. If you could just show us to our suite? We'd really like to get some rest."

"Of course," Mr. Emerson said, turning from me and grabbing the woman's bag. "Right this way."

"Please!" I pleaded. I wanted to say that something had to be done—a barrier put around the nest so it wouldn't be disturbed. The path needed to be kept clear and someone had to see that they made it safely to the ocean. Mr. Emerson could do all that; he was the inn's caretaker after all. But he and the couple were bustling away. There was nothing I could do but watch them go.

For a dizzying moment, I felt like I was free-falling. I wasn't sure where to turn. Dad was thousands of miles away. I no longer had my phone. But I'd given up on relying on others anyway, hadn't I? I didn't want all the complications and expectations that came along with other people's involvement.

But I had to do something about the nest. I thought back to the turtle skeleton Dad and I had found years ago and then to the dozens of eggs buried beneath the sand—buried in a not-so-great location. I couldn't bear for any of them to meet the same fate. I would feel responsible. I was the one who'd knocked out the pool light. Was that the reason the mama turtle had finally come ashore?

There had to be something I could do. I raced home, through the side door of the garage, and then rummaged around until I found a spool of orange twine.

With the twine tucked safely under my arm, I made my way back to the beach and began searching for pieces of driftwood large enough to serve as stakes.

"Whatchadoin?" Lanie's voice rang out, and I jolted, nearly dropping the armful of sticks I'd gathered.

"Shhh, Lanie. You don't want to wake the whole neighborhood." By neighborhood, I meant Mom and our grandparents.

"Can I help?" she asked in a quieter tone.

"Sure. Carry these," I said, and dumped a few pieces of driftwood into her arms.

She followed me back to the nest. I wanted to get the barrier up before the inn's guests started to trickle down to the beach.

It wasn't easy to drive the driftwood into the sand, though. I had to dig holes for the makeshift stakes with my bare hands and find a rock to finish pounding the stakes in.

An early-morning jogger eyed me suspiciously while I was pounding in the last stake. Then I had to move aside to let a large man through the Beachcomber gate as I was winding the twine around the pieces of driftwood now sticking straight out of the sand. But finally I encircled the nest. It wasn't as official looking as I'd hoped, but it would do the trick. It would keep people from disturbing the nest.

"There," I said, feeling a small amount of pride and relief.

"What is it?" Lanie asked. She'd been more helpful than I'd anticipated. Not in the actual building of the barrier, but she had retrieved a pair of scissors for me at one point when I needed to cut the twine.

"It's . . . um . . ." I stalled. If she knew about the eggs, she'd want to spend every waking moment watching for the turtles to hatch. Then, next thing I knew, it would become a family affair. She'd drag my grandparents and mom into staking out the nest. And things would go south, like they always did with my family.

Now that the barrier was up, I was starting to feel better about things. Excited even. The barrier would keep the nest safe. Then sometime between six to eight weeks from now, the eggs would hatch. Up until that moment, I'd been dreading the rest of summer away from Dad, but now I was relieved to know I'd still be in Florida for a while longer. I imagined myself overseeing the hatchlings as they dashed for the waves. Me. Not everyone else crowding in.

"It's . . ." I struggled to come up with a reasonable explanation. "Art?"

Judging by the look on her face, Lanie either wasn't convinced or was sorely disappointed in my work.

I never found out, because as soon as the lie slipped from my lips, Grandma started calling my name. "Olivia! There's someone at the door for you. Olivia?"

If anything could make Lanie forget about the driftwood posts and twine, it was the intrigue of a visitor at the door. She shot off like a rocket, even though Grandma clearly said the guest was for me.

I wasn't all that quick to follow. I expected to find Mr. Emerson at the door, wanting to apologize for having brushed me off again. And, at that point, I was convinced I was better off handling everything alone. No one to please. No one to disappoint. The turtle had finally succeeded in coming ashore. I was done trying to keep Mom happy and fool Dad and my friends into thinking I was having a good time. The only thing I cared about now was protecting the nest.

But it wasn't Mr. Emerson at the door. It was his grandson. And he was holding two sets of snorkel gear in his hands.

15

**Loggerhead hatchlings are a mere
two inches in length.**

The instant I made eye contact with Aiden, it dawned on me that protecting the nest wasn't the *only* thing I cared about. We stared at each other for a zing-filled second, then both looked away.

"Hi," I said shyly, worried what he was thinking after the way we'd last parted.

"Hi," he said back, just as timidly. "My mom dropped me off. She didn't have time to visit Grandpa today, but I really wanted to see you."

My heart soared. Not only was the nest protected, but Aiden had come to see me. He didn't have to come, but he came anyway.

Grandma surprised me by not lingering nearby the way

Aunt Michelle had. In fact, she even lured Lanie into the kitchen with the promise of finding something sweet to eat.

As soon as they were gone, I mumbled an apology. "I didn't mean what I said the other night . . ." My mouth felt dry. I swallowed, then added, "I'm so glad you're here." While I spoke, I kept my eyes bolted to the floor, of course. I didn't think I could handle meeting his gaze a second time.

"Thanks. I thought—" The pitch of Aiden's voice changed. He cleared his throat before continuing. "I thought maybe we could go snorkeling by Bradenton Beach. Your grandma already okayed it. And . . . I brought you something."

I looked up. He'd set the snorkel gear down and was rustling around in his bag. He withdrew an ear of corn. When he held it out to me, his face was as pink as the inside of a conch shell. "Sorry I couldn't bring you one on your birthday. My mom was showing Grandpa how to search for job listings online. I didn't want to bother them with taking me to the store."

"Thank you!" I took the corn from his hands and cradled it in my own. It was cold and still wrapped in the husk. It might've been the sweetest gift I'd ever received. "Let me get changed quick. I'll be right back."

Grandma smiled broadly when I dropped the corn off in the kitchen and thanked her for letting me go snorkeling. She squeezed my hand and told me to "have a wonderful time, dear." My feet were light as I bounded up the stairs and threw on a swimsuit and the cover-up Aunt Michelle had given me for my birthday. I told myself there was no need to worry. The nest would be perfectly fine while I was gone. There was no way the eggs would hatch today—it would be weeks before the turtles would emerge—and no one would disturb the nest with the barrier up. There wasn't anything holding me back.

I practically flew back down the stairs. For the first time since I'd been here, I was leaving the beach house with the sole intent of having fun.

We rode the trolley to the third pier at the south end of Bradenton Beach. It wasn't a historic landmark, like the one on the opposite end of the island that I'd taken a photo of for Dad. And it wasn't surrounded by restaurants and shops, like the nearby Bridge Street Pier. It was basically an old walkway jutting into the ocean. There was a lifeguard tower a short distance away. That had to be part of the reason Grandma was okay with this. I wondered what else might've persuaded her as Aiden and I rode side by side, the flippers resting between our legs so that my right knee kept grazing his left.

"What did you say to my grandma?" I asked.

"Why?" he asked, and drummed his fingers on his lap. When he noticed me noticing, he locked his fingers into fists. "I left my cube at home," he said. It was an incomplete explanation, but I think I understood. The finger-twitching thing was a nervous habit.

"Grandma seemed to be in a weirdly good mood. And it's strange that she agreed to let me go snorkeling so easily. She kinda freaked out when I rode the trolley alone this summer."

Aiden reached into his bag and pulled out a small white tube for me to examine. "I think I might've impressed her with my sunscreen," he said. "I was putting it on when she answered the door."

I read the label. "It's reef friendly?"

"It uses green tea instead of harmful chemicals," Aiden explained. "Your grandma seemed to like that."

I nodded and smiled. "Yeah, that sounds about right."

"And I might've told her she has nice skin."

I shot him a sidelong glance and he shrugged. "What? She does, and I *really* wanted her to let you come."

My flip-flops gathered sand as we made our way from the trolley stop onto the beach. The weathered pier appeared in the distance. Concrete pillars supporting the walkway extended into the ocean, forming underwater nooks and crannies in which schools of fish could hide. Algae and seaweed clung to the pier like fuzzy goatees.

"Race you there!" I said, and took off running. It felt marvelous to pump my legs. I was out of breath but full of life as I reached the pier a few steps ahead of Aiden.

When I glanced back, his head was hung, and he was shaking it side to side.

I tensed. Maybe racing across the sand was something teenagers didn't do. But then Aiden grinned and said, "You beat me here, but I'm gonna beat you to the water." He scrambled into his fins, then ditched his glasses and pulled on his mask like a pro. I wasn't nearly as smooth as I stumbled into mine. When I slipped into the surf, his fins were already slapping the surface in front of me.

Once we were deeper in, beneath the waves, we met face-to-face. Aiden's face lit into a victorious smile behind his mask. I beamed back at him, then we took off swimming.

As we dove and swam around the concrete blocks, breathing through our snorkels, we mostly saw silver mullets and a few sheepsheads.

Sheepshead fish always made me a little uneasy. Not because of their size or because they pose any sort of threat, but because their teeth are humanlike. It was hard to get a good look at their incisors underwater, but a fisherman once showed me a sheepshead he'd caught off the pier. It was like peering into a kid's mouth. Majorly creepy.

Not only that, with all the Forrester Family Fabulous Facts floating around in my head, I recalled that because of the vertical black stripes running down a silvery body, they're often called convict fish. It was an unwelcome reminder of my recent criminal activity.

I veered away from the pier, keeping my mask trained on the shimmery ocean bottom. The way the sunlight shone through the water, it seemed to dance across the sand. I let my body go still—felt the weightlessness as the waves carried me and I rose and dipped with each intake and exhale of air.

Out of the corner of my eye, I caught a glimpse of a young sea turtle soaring by. The way she glided through the water, changing course with a gentle curve of one flipper, made her seem otherworldly. Like a celestial being in a starry sky. I wanted to alert Aiden somehow, so he wouldn't miss her, but he was too far away—still back by the pier. Plus, she was gone nearly as quickly as she'd arrived, another shadow in the murky water beyond where I could see.

The sighting wasn't something I'd been able to share with Aiden or Dad, but maybe the moment was somehow meant to be mine alone. The encounter left me feeling more resolved than ever. I would protect the nest. The hatchlings would one day swim in the ocean.

Aiden and I hardly spoke on the trolley ride back. But something had solidified between us. No matter how much he'd changed on the outside, he was still the same sweet and funny boy I'd spent so many summers with. I knew he didn't feel comfortable confronting his grandpa on my behalf, and I wouldn't ask him to again. But we were friends. Friends who shared thoughts and feelings with one another. That is, when we weren't exhausted from hours spent snorkeling. We didn't need my dad here to glue us together. We were close enough already.

. . .

Mom greeted me at the door like a fresh westerly wind, out of breath and glowing with delight. "Liv! Come to the kitchen. I need your help!"

I should've known Mom would pull some stunt—something to counteract how icily I'd treated her when she confiscated my phone. Still, my curiosity got the better of me and it was impossible not to follow. It'd been a very long time since I'd seen her so flushed with excitement. I had to know the cause.

She had the kitchen draped in drop cloths, and canvases were spread across the floor. She'd been sketching and painting sea life: dolphins and turtles, starfish and shells. They were pretty good. Mom went to college on an art scholarship, but over the last few years, I'd rarely seen her holding a paintbrush. I was glad to see her taking this step. I thought it meant she was getting back to her old self.

My sister was sitting on the floor next to the largest canvas.

It was split down the middle, ocean on one side, beach on the other. Mom had stenciled SEA OF LOVE across the top.

"It's a gift," she said, "for Grandma and Grandma. For letting us stay here." She couldn't stand still—she kept shifting her weight from one foot to the other—and her eyes were practically begging for approval.

Lanie squealed. "Oh, it's so pretty!"

My opinion did a one-eighty when I realized what she was really doing. I set my jaw. Mom wasn't painting for the fun and enjoyment of it. She was up to something else, and I didn't like it.

Bolstered by Lanie's praise, Mom beamed. "I, um, want to add our footprints to the sand." She stopped fidgeting and moved purposefully around the kitchen, pointing out the supplies she'd set up. "See, we'll put paint on the bottoms of our bare feet and stamp them on the canvas. That way, Grandma and Grandpa will think of us every time they look at it."

Think of us—of me, Lanie, and Mom. It was like Mom was in a hurry to rewrite our family's history. Five summers ago, when Lanie was one, she'd given Grandpa and Grandma a framed piece of artwork she made from our handprints. She'd traced Dad's hand, then her own, then mine, then Lanie's—all on different colors of card stock. She'd cut them out and arranged them in order so that each print sat nestled in the next. Above the handprints, she'd stenciled NOTHING SAYS LOVE LIKE FAMILY.

Lanie wouldn't remember making it, but I did. I gritted my teeth. Out of habit, I almost held back, not wanting to upset Mom. Then I remembered I was past that. Whether it made her unhappy or not, I was going to tell her how I felt. "You can't . . . you can't do that!" I stammered. Snorkeling had been a short reprieve from the wreck of my home life, but it all came crashing back full force.

"Do what?" Mom asked. She seemed genuinely bewildered by my outburst.

"Pretend like Dad never existed." I was beyond trying to keep everything together. I was so sick of all the pretenses. "You can't just swap out four handprints for three sets of footprints and erase him from the equation like that. It's not that simple." My voice sounded shrill, even to my own ears.

"Olivia," Mom said softly. "I'm not trying to—" I could tell she hadn't expected her project to backfire so spectacularly. She'd expected me to be a willing participant.

"*Yes*, you are. That's exactly what you're doing. That's why you swept us away on this trip. You want us to forget him. You want us to choose you over him. Are you going to make us move here, too, like Aunt Michelle wants?"

Mom breathed in as if she were sucking up the entire ocean before exhaling. "This isn't about choosing sides," she said at last. "Your dad and I didn't want you to be disappointed. We know how much this trip means to you girls every summer. There are going to be enough other changes down the road. Whether that means moving, I haven't decided yet . . . But we didn't want to take this vacation away from you, too."

She sounded so calm. So unlike Mom. Her words sounded rehearsed again. I would've bet money she'd practiced them a hundred times already this summer, trying to convince herself they were true.

"But you never asked me," I retorted. It was the first time I'd had the nerve to say it. It had taken scheming and disappointment and heartache, and pushing the MOB away, the discovery of the nest, a little peace, and now this ridiculous project for the words to finally work their way out. "You never even asked me if I wanted to come. I don't want to move here, and I don't want to stamp my footprints. I don't even want to be around you!"

I flew out the front door, too angry and fired up to think clearly. With my legs on autopilot, I turned and ran along the side of the house, back to the beach. Back to the nest.

The last few days had been such a roller-coaster ride already. Highs and lows. I craved the peace I had with my nights on the beach, kayaking with Grandpa, and snorkeling with Aiden. I longed for another calm, but that was far from where I was headed.

16

Baby sea turtles have a sharp, temporary egg
tooth at the tip of their beaks called a caruncle.
The bony caruncle helps the hatchlings slice
through the eggshell.

I turned a corner, walked around the dune nearest the Beachcomber, and found a man yanking one of my driftwood posts from the ground. "What do you think you're doing?!" I screeched. "Can't you see there's a nest!"

The man nonchalantly ditched the post and retrieved a walkie-talkie from his belt. That's when I noticed the Beachcomber insignia embroidered above the pocket on his polo shirt. "Mr. Shaw," he spoke into the portable radio, "we have a . . . situation out here. There's a little girl. She doesn't want me to, uh, remove the obstruction."

"Little girl? Obstruction?" I fired back. I was spun as mad as a cyclone from my spat with Mom, and now this?

"I see her," Mr. Shaw's voice boomed over the walkie-talkie. "I'm headed your way."

I whipped around until I spotted the Beachcomber's owner slinking out from under the patio cover. He was wearing that infuriating plastic smile, but the glare in his eyes was extra menacing.

Marching through the gate, I met him halfway. "You can't take it down!" I protested. "It's not an obstruction." A woman reading near the pool lowered her book and stared at us from above her aviator sunglasses.

Mr. Shaw laid his hand gently on my shoulder. "I understand your concern." He was so controlled. So composed. So obviously used to dealing with irate customers.

I shrugged him off.

Mr. Shaw sighed deeply and said, "Let's go see, shall we?" He causally meandered toward the gate and I followed along. I wasn't naive this time. I knew he was moving us out of range of any eavesdroppers, but I went along with it because we were headed to the nest.

Once we'd exited the pool area and the woman went back to her book, he said, "Why do you think people visit Anna Maria Island?" Without missing a beat, he answered his own question. "To relax and enjoy the white, sandy beaches."

Then, as we came upon the worker with the portable radio,

he dismissed him. "Thanks, Alex," he said. "I can take it from here."

Alex nodded and left, and it was only me and Mr. Shaw standing over the nest and my half-removed barrier. It was uncomfortable, but I refused to be intimidated. I'd learned my lesson. He wouldn't chase me off again.

"People might say they come for the wildlife—the manatees, dolphins, and sea turtles—but that's true only so long as they aren't inconvenienced by them. Your average vacationer doesn't want to pick up trash or forgo his disposable plastic bottle for the sake of the marine life.

"This thing you've put up . . . It's cute. I'm sure your intentions are good. But what happens if one of my guests wants to bring a wagon down this path? He'd have to go around the front of the inn and down a few blocks to find public beach access." Mr. Shaw spoke haughtily as if explaining all of this to a much younger child. "What good is beachfront property if the path to the ocean is obstructed? Do you think tourists would rather have memories and photos of this garbage"—he pointed at my barrier—"or of the clean, pristine beaches we promise our guests?"

"I think they'd want the baby turtles to live," I said stubbornly.

Mr. Shaw frowned. His perfectly coifed hair stood its

ground against the strong ocean breeze. My hair was blowing all over the place. I pulled it away from my eyes, and Mr. Shaw said, "You have a . . . *distinctive* face."

I wasn't sure what he meant by that, but it sounded like an insult. Before I could show him how distinctive my scowl could be, he added, "Our security camera captured some interesting footage the night the light was broken. I reviewed it after you confessed and, sure enough, there you are, clear as day, vandalizing my property. I decided to hold on to the video in case you started stirring up trouble again." He raised his eyebrows. "Glad I did."

My face froze. My insides turned glacial. Just when I'd decided to start speaking my mind, my voice box plummeted to the pit of my stomach.

"How about this? I take down the posts. You don't tell anyone about this nest, and I won't turn the video of my property being damaged over to the authorities." Mr. Shaw was smiling again—a bright toothpaste-ad-worthy smile. "Deal?"

What would Dad think if I got in trouble with the police? What would Aunt Michelle say if she heard I'd been charged with a crime? That she told me so? I must've taken too long to consider because the smile faded from Mr. Shaw's face, and he said, "Don't try me. If it comes to it, the eggs will be gone. Get my drift?"

"You can't do that!" I balked. "It's illegal to disturb a nest."

"Tell me this: If there aren't any eggs to be found, who's to say there was ever a nest here. You? A girl visiting from out of state that saw, what? A patch of sand that looked slightly different than the rest of the beach?" Mr. Shaw snickered. "*Please*, like that's proof of anything. The video, on the other hand . . . So what do you say? The posts go away, we pretend there's nothing but a path here, and we both go on about our lives."

I took a deep breath before responding. "You promise you'll leave the eggs alone."

"Sheesh," he wheezed. "Scout's honor, or whatever it is kids say these days."

"And the lights on the Beachcomber?" I pressed. "Will you make them turtle friendly?"

"You're kidding, right? Don't push your luck, kid. Really, you have nothing to bargain with here. If anything, I'm doing you a favor."

I took my time but, at last, I said, "Okay." I hated myself for giving in, but what choice did I have?

"What was that?"

"I said, *okay*."

He broke back into a toothy grin. "See there. It isn't so hard to be a good neighbor." He clapped me on the back before ripping the remaining posts out of the sand. Then he carried my barrier with him through the gate. He whistled as he made his way toward the inn.

17

Hatchlings typically choose to emerge from the nest during the night.

If Lanie thought I had a shell at the beginning of the summer, it was nothing compared to the days and weeks after I made the deal with Mr. Shaw. I had more reason than ever to hide in my room. It was easier to separate myself from everyone than pretend everything was fine.

I promised Mr. Shaw I wouldn't tell anyone about the nest. I had to keep that promise or the eggs would be gone. My silence didn't mean I couldn't keep an eye on it, though. Every night, I snuck out to my spot between the dunes. I collected pieces of sea glass. And when it was quiet next door, I walked down the beach and inspected the sand near the Beachcomber's gate for any signs of change. Then I cleared the path of chairs and umbrellas that had been forgotten on the beach. Each morning, I returned to see if the eggs had hatched and to make sure the nest hadn't been disturbed.

After a while, something odd caught my attention—one night a week, the Beachcomber went dark. The light I'd broken had quickly been replaced, but on Tuesdays after sunset, it was turned off. So were the rest of the outdoor lights on the Beachcomber's property.

I figured Mr. Emerson was doing what he could to help since he was the only person who knew about the nest besides me and Mr. Shaw. It was a nice thought, but what were the chances the eggs would hatch on a Tuesday?

When Aiden was around, we fell into a steady rhythm. I listened to him talk about an upcoming Rubik's tournament and how he'd shaved another ten seconds off his best time. After we'd gone snorkeling, he was more himself around me. Playful and kind. But he grew serious every time he spoke about his grandpa. He feared Mr. Shaw was only keeping Mr. Emerson on until the end of summer.

As the weeks came and went, I was engulfed by island time. It happened every summer. Dad always said it was like living in a vacuum where things passed by sort of slow and fast all at once. Slow because everything happened at a leisurely pace, and fast because, before you knew it, entire months had gone by in the blink of an eye.

Mom and Lanie were lulled into it, too. That might've been the reason Mom never gave my phone back—she lost track of time. But it's not like I asked for it, either. My phone was a link to my old life, my friends, my dad. But with everything else, I couldn't keep up the charade with them, too. The facade that I was having fun and living a carefree life in Florida was too much work.

Summer seemed endless. Day after day, nothing really changed. And then it did—on the Friday Grandma and Grandpa took Lanie to Disney World. They'd held my sister off for most of the summer—a remarkable feat. I think they were hoping I'd give in and come along, too.

"Are you sure you won't come, Olivia?" Grandpa asked. "It won't be the same without you."

Grandma chimed in. "How can you say no to the Magic Kingdom?"

It wasn't as hard as they thought. The Magic Kingdom didn't seem very magical anymore. I hardly wanted to visit an amusement park with a happily-ever-after theme. If storybook endings were what made it the happiest place on earth, then clearly it wasn't for our family. My sister just didn't know that yet.

Mom bowed out, too. She said the rides made her sick. But I think it might've been the thought of all the princesses and their handsome princes vowing eternal love for each other that turned her stomach.

My grandparents and Lanie got an early start. It was a two-hour drive from Anna Maria Island, and they wanted to be there when the gates opened. I was still in bed when I heard them leave.

Within five minutes of their departure, I was down on the beach. The ocean air had a decidedly fishy smell as I walked along the edge of the surf. Bits of seaweed had washed ashore. I hopped over the strands of green and brown. I was so pre-occupied with avoiding the seaweed that it wasn't until I was practically on top of the nest that I noticed something was different.

A shallow hole.

Tiny tracks leading toward the ocean.

My heart simultaneously celebrated and grieved. I hadn't expected it to happen this soon, but the incubation period could vary by as much as two weeks. The turtles had emerged from the nest. I had missed it.

The whole thing felt, I don't know, somewhat anticlimactic. This had been my sole purpose for most of the summer, and now it was over. At least I'd been diligent in clearing their path the night before.

I sighed and smiled wistfully as I examined the little tread marks, like miniature tire tracks, leading to the ocean. I pictured the burst of hatchlings breaking through the sand. I'd read at the aquarium that the eruption is called a boil. It happens so suddenly, and with dozens of baby turtles rising, it appears the sand is boiling.

Then teeny turtle flippers flip-flop over and over, pushing the hatchlings forward just a wee bit with each stroke. I pictured their trek to the water, flippers furiously pounding the sand. What a sight it must've been. I thought of the mama turtle I'd seen my first few nights on the island and hoped she knew her nest had been a success—that her babies were swimming in the ocean.

I sighed a second time, then turned to leave. As I swung around toward the beach house, I noticed a few tiny tracks leading the way I'd come. I'd been too lost in thought to notice before, but I must've walked right over them.

The blood in my veins turned to ice. Some of the hatchlings had gone the wrong way. They'd gone inland instead of to the ocean. I took a deep breath and tried to remain calm. Even though they'd probably been digging their way out for days, they'd chosen last night to emerge. They might still be alive. This was why I'd made it my mission to check on the nest daily. I couldn't fail them.

I bent over to inspect the wayward tracks. They veered

away from the beach, zigzagging into the dunes. I tried to follow, but the tracks ended where the seaweed and grasses began. The lost hatchlings could've wandered deeper into the dunes in either direction. They could've wandered to the street even. They could be anywhere and there were too many places to search on my own.

Panic tingled inside me—from the top of my head to the tips of my toes. All along I'd thought I'd be enough. I'd thought I could protect the nest and hatchlings without assistance from anyone else. But, as much as I hated to admit it, now that the time had come, I needed help.

I cursed Mom for taking my phone. I had no idea where she'd stashed it. I sprinted for the house. The sand drank my toes and drew my feet in with every step. I fought against the drag and forced myself to keep running.

I threw open the door to the beach house. "Mom!" I screamed. It had been a very long time since I'd called for her. It had been a very long time since I'd spoken more than a few words in her presence, but she was there in a heartbeat.

"Olivia, what is it? What's wrong, baby?"

With Mr. Shaw's threat to get rid of the eggs no longer hanging over me, I swallowed my resentment and told her everything.

18

Hatchlings work as a team to break free from the nest. Instinct tells them which way is up as they burrow together to get through more than two feet of hard-packed sand.

After I finished explaining what I'd found, I told Mom to call the aquarium. I knew they'd handled turtle rescues before and could give us guidance. I paced back and forth in the kitchen, anxious to get started while Mom did a lot of nodding and saying "uh-huh" into her cell. When she finally clicked it off, she told me to grab a towel from the closet while she grabbed a bucket and some other tools from the garage.

Before we parted, she said the aquarium was sending someone from their sea turtle conservation and research program to assist us, but the hatchlings might need our help before the woman arrived. They'd given us permission to handle the turtles if we carefully followed their instructions.

Once I had the towel and Mom had the other items, we met up behind the house. I quickly led Mom to the place where the hatchlings had erupted from the nest. She scooped sand with a hand shovel into the bucket while I raced to the ocean and returned with a cup full of water. We dampened the sand in the bucket, then headed in the direction of the tracks. We'd been searching the dunes for five or ten minutes when I discovered a tiny hatchling writhing around in the underbrush. His flippers beat the ground like drums. He was hung up on the stem of a plant.

Mom held the stem back while I carefully lifted the hatchling away from the shrub, before gently nestling him in the wet sand. We draped the towel over the top of the bucket and kept searching. By the time the lady from the conservation and research program arrived, we'd rescued two more baby turtles. They all seemed on the brink of exhaustion—their movements were slow and defeated rather than the hard, fast strokes baby turtles usually make.

It took me a minute to place the young woman sent to help. She was wearing a sun hat and glasses, but I knew I'd seen her somewhere before. Then it hit me: She was the tour guide from the kayaking expedition I took with Grandpa.

"You're . . ." I trailed off, racking my brain for her name.

"Sarah!" she finished for me. "And you're a budding

ecologist. Olivia, right? I remember you and your grandfather. We saw some really cool birds that day."

"But you're a kayaking guide, and college student," I said, not even trying to mask my astonishment.

Sarah chuckled. "Yep, and I volunteer for the conservation. I'm a busy gal. Now, let me see the hatchlings." Sarah moved toward the bucket. She lifted the towel and peered inside. "Aw, poor little guys," she said. "Looks like you were rescued just in time! Let's see if any of your brothers and sisters still need a hand, shall we?"

I followed Sarah as she hunted the dunes for more hatchlings. Mom stayed with the bucket, keeping an eye on the ones we'd already found.

"So, you live here, on the island?" Sarah asked. I'd been impressed by her last time we'd met. Now that I knew she rescued turtles, too, I was bursting with admiration. The kind that made me worried I'd make a fool out of myself.

"No, visiting my grandparents for the summer," I said, trying to control the waver in my voice.

Sarah kept the conversation going as we continued to search. "Just you and your mom?"

"And my little sister, Lanie," I added quickly.

"Ah," Sarah said.

Somehow that short, little word opened the floodgates.

"My parents are getting divorced" spilled out of my mouth before I could think better of it. It was only the second time I'd said it aloud. The first time had been to Aiden. I guess it was good to get the practice. I knew it wouldn't be the last time I'd have to say it. This near stranger, someone who'd never met my dad, and wouldn't ask me if I was all right or why my parents had separated, suddenly seemed like the perfect person to have divulged this bit of information to. At the same time, I was mortified I'd shared something so personal with her. Her life seemed perfect, and mine clearly wasn't.

"Mine are divorced, too," Sarah said, not missing a beat. She raised her eyes from the dunes and flashed me a knowing smile. "Happened when I was about your age," she said, then went back to scouring the underbrush.

It was reassuring to know someone who seemed so on top of everything had once been where I was now. "And?" I asked, hoping I didn't sound too needy, or weird.

"And it was awful. My parents couldn't stand to be in the same room, or even be decent enough to each other when they talked on the phone. They still can't, so I became the intermediary. They tell me to pass along messages—not all of them are very nice. They make me work out their scheduling conflicts, stuff like that."

"Oh," I said. "That does sound awful."

"It's different for everyone. But I think it's hard and sad no matter what. It made me grow up fast, you know?"

I nodded my head, even though I wasn't sure I did.

"In the long run, the whole thing made me a better, stronger person." Sarah paused and then glanced at my mom standing across the beach with her hand shielding her eyes from the sun. She was watching us, or maybe she was just watching me. "It's good that you and your mom are close."

"Um, yeah, thanks," I said self-consciously. "I guess." Mom and I weren't close. Lanie and Mom were close, but Sarah hadn't seen the two of them together.

"Aha!" Sarah said. For a second, I was worried she was calling me out on my lie. Then she lifted a squirming hatchling from the dune. "Got you!" We brought the hatchling to the bucket and reunited it with its siblings. After that, Sarah didn't talk anymore about her parents, and I didn't talk anymore about mine.

We searched the dunes for several more hours, but only came across one more hatchling. When we set them free, Sarah demonstrated where to release the baby turtles. She turned them toward the ocean and placed them not quite in the surf. One by one, the hatchlings with heads so big they seemed wobbly scrambled across the sand with fierce determination. They no longer seemed exhausted as they raced for the sea and got tossed by the first few waves. I found myself whispering a prayer as the ocean gobbled each one of them whole.

"Only one in a thousand makes it to adulthood," Sarah said, and I was reminded of Dad saying the exact same thing. "They still have a rough road ahead of them—they'll have to escape predators and fishermen—but their chances for survival just got a whole lot better, thanks to you."

Mom wrapped her arm around my shoulder and squeezed. Moved by what we'd just been a part of, I settled into her embrace.

Sarah gave us the number for the island's turtle watch before she left. "If you stumble across another nest, they'll mark it off and keep it monitored. It's run by volunteers. You two might think about joining—you already have experience. Oh, and they also walk the beach once a week to check for any lighting-ordinance violations."

Something about what Sarah said nagged at me as Mom and I walked back to the beach house. But I was so jazzed about saving the hatchlings that I couldn't concentrate. And then Mom said, "That was amazing. You did great."

"Thanks," I said. And I felt great. All afternoon my mind kept replaying the image of the rescued hatchlings racing for the waves. Every time I pictured their flippers slapping the sand, I smiled to myself and my heart hummed a happy tune.

Lanie and my grandparents still weren't back when my stomach started growling for food. "They're staying for the parade," Mom informed me. "Grandma called a little bit ago. I guess we're on our own for dinner."

I felt a tug, pulling me back, telling me to retreat into my room again. Mom and me sharing a meal, just the two of us? No, thank you. But then I thought of the way she'd sprung into action when I needed her help, and I figured it might not be that bad.

We decided to order a pizza.

"What kind do you want?" I asked.

"You know, I'm not sure." Mom laughed, but it didn't sound like a laugh. It sounded sad and hollow. "I've forgotten what I like."

Back home we always ordered a cheese pizza, because that was mine and Lanie's favorite, and a sausage and black olive, because that's what Dad liked.

We finally settled on half cheese for me, half ham and green pepper for Mom.

It was too awkward to wait in the same room as Mom for the pizza to arrive. But after the doorbell rang and I followed my nose back to the kitchen, I found the table set for two. As much as I wanted to grab a few slices and ghost, the thought of Mom eating alone at the neatly set table was too depressing.

She smiled when I slid into the seat next to hers. "I hope Lanie isn't wearing your grandparents out," she confided in me. "She's a bit spirited, and they're . . ."

"Old," I offered.

Mom laughed, a sincere laugh this time. "I was looking for a politer way to phrase it, but, yeah, they're old. Your sister wears *me* out sometimes."

"Me too," I said.

I could probably count on one hand the number of times Mom and I had spent an evening together, just her and me. It might happen more often now. What would that be like?

It's not like Dad had never missed a dinner with the family. But the house would feel so much emptier without his coffee mug set out for breakfast the next day or his sweater hanging on the coatrack. Even when he wasn't there, there had always been reminders of him everywhere. He'd probably cleared those things out weeks ago. That was the plan. He'd finish moving out while we were in Florida and while he was on break between semesters.

I pictured the empty side of his and Mom's closet and all the books missing from the office shelves. Thinking about home made my throat feel tight. But now that the nest had hatched, what was there to distract me from thoughts of Dad and my family's future? I felt an urgent need to leave the suffocating space inside the kitchen with my mother. Out on the beach, I knew I'd feel better.

"Um . . ." I hesitated. Leaving abruptly didn't seem right, but I hadn't asked for permission to go outside a single time all summer. "I'm done eating, and I was thinking I'd go . . ." I trailed off.

Mom's mouth twisted into an unreadable expression. She sighed and nodded her head. "Sure," she said. "Just be careful out there. There's a high riptide warning for tonight. Stay out of the water."

I began to leave. As an afterthought, I turned and said, "Thanks, Mom. Thanks for helping me rescue the hatchlings, and for dinner, and for not making a fuss over me going to the beach after dark."

She got a sappy, far-off look on her face, like me showing a little gratitude might make her cry. So I sped out of there like a hatchling racing for the water.

The usual breeze was far more than a breeze that night. It lifted my hair and each blast felt gritty, pelting my skin with sand. I darted for the sheltered space between my dunes.

The Beachcomber had been gnawing at my thoughts all day. I knew exactly why those baby turtles had become disoriented and headed the wrong direction. Then there was what Sarah had said about the turtle watch keeping an eye out for lighting violations. But it made me so mad, I couldn't bear to think about it. I focused instead on the fact that we'd found the hatchlings.

I combed my fingers through the sand, expecting to find a piece of sea glass, but came up empty. It bugged me that one wasn't there. A mermaid tear had always been waiting for me. I still wasn't sure where they were coming from, but I'd come to expect them. I wanted another to add to my collection. Scooting to my hands and knees, I scoured the surrounding area. When I didn't find the piece of sea glass in the sand, I moved to the grassy area just beyond.

It wasn't long before my hands located something unusual in the weeds. I recoiled at the touch. It wasn't the smooth, cool, hard texture of glass that I'd anticipated. Whatever it was, it was much larger than a mermaid tear—bumpy and squishy, too.

I quickly spread the grasses apart. In the moonlight, I made out the oblong shape of a tiny shell. But unlike the other hatchlings, when I lifted this sweet baby turtle in my hand, his too-large head drooped, and his flippers hung at his sides.

My heart shattered. We'd missed one, and for this little guy, it was too late. The day's heat had been too much. He was gone.

I lifted my head. My razor-sharp line of sight zoomed in on the Beachcomber. I breathed in steeply through my nose. My chin quivered. My eyes stung. My chest heaved and ached.

The poor hatchling was dead, and it was all Mr. Shaw's fault.

19

When sea turtle hatchlings surface from the nest, they open their eyes for the very first time.

I sat there for the longest time with the dead sea turtle cradled in my hand. "I'm sorry," I whispered. But it wasn't enough. It wasn't near enough. I was tired of meaningless apologies. How many times had I heard *I'm sorry* this summer? From Mom, from Dad, from my grandparents, from Aiden, and from Lanie. Even the twins apologized when they'd ruined my birthday breakfast. And I'd said it more than a few times myself. But what difference did it make? Everyone went right on hurting one another. And nothing ever changed.

I felt helpless and sick to my stomach as all the feelings of grief and melancholy, and resentment, and anger, and everything, *everything* I'd been pushing deep down inside this summer rose like bile in my throat. The hurt felt too big to contain.

I sprang to my feet and frantically searched the area near the dunes once more. It took less than a minute to find what I was looking for—a wide, smooth piece of driftwood in the dunes. Carrying it with me to the water's edge, I settled the lifeless hatchling in a knotty, hollowed-out area of the wood. The waves were rough, but the driftwood was wide enough to stay afloat as I pushed the tiny vessel out to sea.

As I watched the hatchling get carried off by moonlit water, I shivered. But it wasn't from the cold. All the emotions running through me were causing me to quake. I hugged myself, trying to stop the tremors while walking up the shoreline, past the dunes, back toward the beach house.

"Liv?" My sister appeared on the path as I reached the back door. A sparkly pink tiara was painted on her forehead, and her cheeks had been blasted with color and sprinkled with pixie dust. She gripped the string of a yellow balloon with mouse ears as the wind tried to tease it free from her hand. Grandma and Grandpa had gone all out to give her a magical day.

"Liv?" she said again. "What are you doing?"

With her big gray-green eyes, wavy hair, and fancifully decorated face, she looked as though she belonged in a fairy tale.

"Leave me alone, Lanie," I croaked.

She noticed the tears teeming in my eyes and immediately pulled the lettered olive out of her pocket and drew it toward her lips.

That small action of hers was what finally did me in. The dam inside me snapped. The pressure had been building and building. I couldn't hold it in any longer. "Stop it, Lanie. Just stop," I pleaded, my voice hoarse and raw with emotion. "Wishing isn't going to change anything," I said. "It isn't going to make me happy or bring Dad and Mom back together. THAT is what you've been wishing for all summer, isn't it?"

Lanie's face crumbled. I'd struck gold with that one. All her secretive whispering into the shell, her unshakable cheeriness . . . The reason she'd been unfazed by everything was because she truly believed things would magically go back to the way they were before.

"Fairy tales aren't real, Lanie." I hugged myself tighter. "I wish they were, but even when you think things are going to be okay"— I thought back to how happy I'd been after rescuing the other hatchlings—"something terrible happens that ruins everything." Nothing would ever bring back the baby sea turtle, and nothing would fix our family. "Our family is broken," I said, "and wishes don't put broken things back together."

Lanie gasped and at the same time a sudden gust finally teased the balloon free from her hand. The wind whipped it toward the ocean. She snatched for the string and the yellow mouse ears, and the lettered olive teetered from her fingers. It shattered when it hit the concrete. Balloon forgotten, she immediately hunched over and tried to collect the sharp fragments of her wishing shell.

"Oh, Lanie, let me help you," I said. I lowered myself to the ground beside her, full of regret for being so blunt.

Anguish puddled in my sister's eyes and a whimper gurgled in her throat. "No," she said. "Maybe *you're* the something terrible that ruins everything."

Ouch, I thought. Maybe she was right. Everything that had gone wrong lately had one common ingredient—me. I slowly rose to my feet. I'd failed the turtles and Mom and Dad, I'd caused a rift between Mom and Aunt Michelle, and now I'd failed Lanie. If I was being honest, I'd been failing her all summer—chasing her off the beach and telling her scary stories to keep her away. She was the one person I hadn't made much effort to please.

Grandma and Grandpa were coming up the path. I could almost hear their joints creaking, but they didn't slow down. I wasn't sure how much of the outburst they'd heard, but from the pinched expression on Grandma's face, I could tell they'd heard enough. I couldn't take it if Grandma, or worse, Grandpa, tsked at me or asked me what I had done. Lanie was upset and that meant I had failed them, too.

I fled to my room.

I crawled into bed with my clothes on and stared up at the ceiling. My tongue swelled in my mouth and my teeth bit together around it, but there was too much guilt and grief for me to swallow. When my sister knocked on my door a few minutes later, I didn't answer.

"Liv," she spoke softly through the door. "I didn't mean it. You're not terrible." She waited a long, silent moment, then said, "Come down to the beach with me. Please?"

I shook my head at the door but didn't voice my response. Going to the beach with her would make things worse. I'd say or do something wrong. I'd ruin things again. I rolled over in bed, faced the wall, and listened until I heard her footsteps padding away. I drifted off with hot tears running down my cheeks.

I don't know exactly what woke me. Maybe it was my name spoken in the wind, or a stirring in my heart. Something brought me to the window, though, just a short while after I'd fallen asleep. My eyes felt puffy and swollen from the tears I'd shed. I wiped the sleep from them and stared down at the beach.

A girl walked below my window, her pale tresses afloat and her creamy-white nightgown billowing. For a moment, I wondered if I was still dreaming. She descended upon my secret spot between the dunes. Like a wispy young sapling, she bent with the wind. One hand reached for the sand and she let something slip from her fingertips.

The girl was all long limbs beneath the flowing white fabric, and it occurred to me that she wasn't a vision. Lanie had sprouted over the summer. She'd grown into her body, leaving some of the clumsiness behind. How much she'd changed had escaped me until then, when my foggy head cleared.

I fretted to myself. No matter how much she'd grown, she shouldn't be on the beach alone. When I didn't agree to go with her, I thought she'd go to Mom's room and go to bed, not outdoors. As I was watching her out the window, Lanie reacted to something I couldn't see. She startled, then dashed for the swelling waves.

I pressed my hand to the window. "Lanie, what are you doing?" I said. She'd been practicing a little this summer but still wasn't a strong swimmer. And the ocean was an angry beast tonight.

Shedding the last dregs of sleep, I lunged for the door. When I swung it open, I noticed a note resting on the hardwood floor. It must've been slipped into my room as I slept. It was written in Lanie's lopsided handwriting.

Our Family is:
1. ~~Broken~~
2. Sea Glass

I didn't have the time or care to give her note any thought. The sight of my sister headed for the storming sea was taking up too much space inside my head. As big a pain as she could be, I couldn't bear the thought of something happening to her. I should've gone with her when she asked, or at least warned her not to leave the house by herself.

By the time my bare feet reached soft sand and I could feel the ocean spray on my face, my sister had disappeared. "Lanie!" I screamed into the wind. "Lanie, where are you?"

I turned circles, scanning the beach and then the waves. They rose and dipped, blocking my view. "Lanie!" I screamed again.

When I saw the white fabric of her nightgown coasting on an inky-black wave, terror coursed through me. My throat went dry and my heart drummed louder than the gusting wind. I knew I should go for help, but I also knew if I lost sight of Lanie's nightgown, I'd never be able to find it again in the white-tipped waves. Without a moment's hesitation, I ran and dove headfirst into the ocean.

The water slapped my face and the salty sea stung my skin. I surfaced and gulped for air as a wave washed over me. I choked down a teacup's worth of ocean water. After the wave moved on, I coughed and hacked until I nearly vomited.

It was all I could do to keep my head above the next rolling whitecap, let alone find my sister. Breakers arrived one after the other, swirling me around and dumping me farther from the shore.

I lost track of the beach, the house, even the moon. The ocean engulfed me with its powerful arms and was pulling me in—into the dark, immense abyss. My entire body ached from the struggle. I grew tired. Tired of the messiness of my life. Tired of being so helpless. I couldn't save the hatchling. I couldn't save my sister. I couldn't even save myself.

Bits of my life flickered through my mind like scenes from a movie. I saw my dad sitting alone in his apartment. My mom crying in the pantry. Mr. Emerson's pained expression. Mr. Shaw's plastic smile. Lanie picking up the pieces of her lettered olive. And I didn't want to see any of it anymore. Some things, like the ocean, were too big to fight.

I stopped thrashing, stopped struggling to keep my head above the waves. I let the current take me. The ocean was bone-chillingly cold. My body felt numb. The movies in my head stopped playing and my thoughts became jumbled and disconnected. And then . . . then my hand brushed against something warm. Warm and familiar. Familiar like my favorite song, and the pillow on my bed back home.

I reached out and wrapped my fingers around my sister's rail of an arm. By some miracle, we had drifted together in the big, wide sea. For a moment, I just held on, letting myself be dragged along beside her. The rough waters jostled and jarred, whipping my arm and shoulder, but I refused to let the ocean current tear us apart.

Then, somewhere deep in my gut, a spark of grit and determination torched into a flame. I mustered the strength to pull my sister close. I encircled her torso with my arm and kicked my legs ferociously.

One of Dad's Forrester Family Fabulous Facts came to me when I needed it most: If you ever get caught in a riptide, swim parallel to the shore and escape the current.

I'd been fighting the tide head on. It wasn't a battle I could win, but that didn't mean I couldn't find my way around it.

20

Loggerhead hatchlings who survive the perilous trek to the ocean drift amid the brown seaweed for some time, using it for both cover and food.

When I reached a place where the current ebbed, I swam at an angle toward the beach. I forced myself to ignore the way Lanie's head drooped like the hatchling's had and the way her body hung limp beneath my arm. I focused only on getting her to shore.

She felt heavier when we reached land. I was bone-tired and battered. I could barely find the energy to lug her across the sand, safely beyond the violent surf.

My lungs burned as I screamed for help. Lanie's skin had turned a disturbing shade of gray. Her normally pink-blossom lips had faded to an ugly, sickly blue.

I screamed again and didn't recognize my own voice. The

sound that rose from deep within my stomach sounded more animal than human.

I gripped my sister's hand in mine, and it felt cold. I pressed my lips to her forehead and whispered wishes and prayers into her wet, tangled hair. "Come back, Lanie, please. I'm so, so sorry." I hated that I could do nothing more than utter another worthless apology.

Then someone was beside me, gently nudging me out of the way. My stomach lurched when I saw it was Mr. Emerson.

"I called 911 when I heard you screaming," he said calmly. "I can help."

After I gave a quick nod and moved out of the way, he carefully turned Lanie's chin to one side and drew his ear close to her face. He flipped her reedy, limp wrist and checked for a pulse. The frown on his face sent a dagger straight through my heart.

With the palm of his wrinkled hand, he rapidly pressed down on her chest. In the distance, sirens blared. I willed them toward us. A light inside Grandma and Grandpa's beach house flicked on.

Things were happening so quickly yet taking an eternity. I found myself clasping Lanie's icy fingers but didn't remember taking hold of her hand. A tear fell on her ashen skin, but I hadn't known I was crying. Mr. Emerson didn't stop the lifesaving efforts, but with each passing second my hopes dwindled.

Then, suddenly, Lanie was coughing and choking and making gurgling noises. The blue of her lips faded to gray, then bloomed with pink. Her eyes blinked open and she was staring right at me. Her eyes seem glazed at first, but gradually came into focus.

"Olivia," she croaked. My name never sounded so sweet. "The turtle," she said, her voice raspy and strained.

"Shhh," I tried to soothe. I thought she meant the dead hatchling. How did she know about that? "He's gone," I said. "I . . . I sent him off on a piece of driftwood."

"No." My sister shook her head. "My balloon. The turtle." She still sounded croaky and she broke into tears. Rivulets ran down her cheeks and landed in the sand beneath her head.

"Lanie, you're not making any sense. Just rest. The ambulance will be here soon." I kissed her forehead, relieved to find it more tepid than before.

"Please, Liv," she said. "I don't want the turtle to die."

Mr. Emerson stood and huffed, his gaze fixed on something in the ocean I couldn't see.

"What is it with you girls and those turtles?" Then, just like that, he took off for the waves. Dazed, I watched him wade chest deep into the raging sea. He squared his body to each incoming swell and was stout enough to somehow keep his footing. But as he worked his way deeper, a violent surge gobbled him up. I held my breath until I saw his head pop above the waves a few seconds later.

"Why?" I said. "What is he doing?" It was all I could do to pull Lanie from the ocean. There was no way I had the strength to rescue Aiden's grandfather.

"Look!" Lanie said, pulling herself to a seated position. "He has her." As she rose, so did more of the ocean inside her. She coughed and sputtered. I feared she'd taken in so much, it might never fully empty out.

When I turned to look, Mr. Emerson was half swimming, half trudging back to the beach. Under one arm, he was lugging a small adult sea turtle. A deflated yellow balloon trailed behind them in the ocean. It wasn't until they came ashore that I put the pieces together. It was Lanie's balloon. The turtle was entangled by the string. That's why she'd gone into the ocean.

Everything happened at once then. The paramedics arrived. They swarmed my sister with instruments—listening to her heart, listening to her breathing, putting tubes in her nose. They were loading her onto a gurney when my mom, grandmother, and grandfather all showed up with bathrobes and stricken expressions. They were so concerned with Lanie, they hardly noticed me.

I squeezed my sister's hand as the rest of my family hovered over her and the paramedics. "Go," she said to me. "I'm okay."

Mr. Emerson was sitting on the edge of the ocean with the turtle overflowing from his lap. The balloon string wrapped around the turtle's head, around its shell, and ensnared its flippers.

"Probably thought she was dining on jellyfish," Mr. Emerson said. "Got an unpleasant surprise tonight, didn't you?" He stared deep into the turtle's eye. "You and me both."

We were both sopping wet, and Mr. Emerson noticed me shivering in the breeze. "What a miserable night," he said, and pulled a pocketknife from his wet cargo pants. "I'll be lucky if it doesn't rust."

He flipped open a silver blade, and it shimmered in the moonlight. With the same care and precision he'd shown in aiding my sister, he sliced through the string, cutting the sea turtle free. The yellow balloon fell to the sand, and I snatched it up and tucked it under a rock before it could blow away again.

"You want to do the honors?" Mr. Emerson asked, staggering under the weight of the turtle as he rose to his feet. She was nearly as big around as a manhole cover and, judging by the way he struggled to lift her, weighed about the same.

"I . . ."

"Well, do you?" He gestured with the turtle, and I met her

gaze. Her eyes watched me with interest. Was she the same turtle I'd seen all those nights before? She looked changed somehow. Not quite as melancholy. More at peace, but still filled with longing. I wondered if she was thinking the same about me.

I nodded my head. Mr. Emerson eased her into my outstretched arms, bearing the brunt of her weight with one hand on her underbelly, another atop her bumpy shell. If she'd squirmed or tried to get away, it would've toppled me. But she seemed to sense that we were returning her to the ocean.

The skin on the bottom sides of her flippers and the place where her neck and head met was a yellowish brown and felt rough like the skin on Grandpa's hands. The plates of her shell were much, much harder and, along with the scales on her head and flippers, had a reddish-brown hue. She was the most majestic creature I'd ever seen.

"Yep. She's a beaut, isn't she?" Mr. Emerson said as if reading my mind.

We carried her into the surf, and I ignored the cold leeching through my already-wet clothes. When the water was up to my waist and mid-thigh on Mr. Emerson, we tipped the sea turtle forward, felt the water receive her weight, and gently let her go. She dipped beneath the waves, her mighty front flippers propelling her into the vast, churning sea.

21

Loggerhead turtles serve as important habitats
to small plants and animals. They carry the
tiny colonies on their shells.

Mom rode with Lanie in the ambulance. The nearest hospital was on the mainland, and the paramedics said there wasn't room for all of us. I stayed behind with my grandparents. Grandma insisted I take a hot bath, put on dry clothes, and go straight to bed. I did what she said, even though I didn't feel much like doing anything. My body begged for rest, but my mind was spinning again like a whirring boat propeller.

When I did drift off, my dreams were mangled images of the limp, dead hatchling and Lanie's lifeless body when I'd dragged her from the ocean. I woke with a cry in my throat. Sleep was out of the question after that.

I crept downstairs, hair wet, wearing the warmest

clothes I'd brought with me to Florida—sweatpants and a soft faded-blue hoodie. The light coming from the kitchen cheered me slightly. I'd spent the last few weeks trying to avoid my family, and now the last thing I wanted was to be by myself.

Grandpa was baking lemon crumb muffins. Stringy gray hairs, normally combed backward, crisscrossed and stuck up from his balding head. He said he couldn't sleep, either, and wanted something to bring with us to visit Lanie at the hospital the next day. "Baking always soothes my spirit, and muffins are all-around heartening, don't you think?"

I nodded my head in agreement and fought back tears. I'd cried too much already, and now seemed like a silly time. Lanie was going to be okay. It was just that the day, the summer, it had all been too much.

"Aw, Liv, come here." Grandpa opened his arms to me. I hesitated for only a moment, then barreled straight into his embrace. He stroked my hair, and my tears fell onto his shoulder and dampened his white undershirt. He smelled like beach wood and kitchen spices that tingled my nose. "You are a smart, brave girl, but not a one of us is strong enough to do this thing called life alone."

Grandma stumbled into the kitchen then, took one look at

us, and headed straight for the pantry. She came out clutching hot cocoa packets to her chest. "If none of us are going to sleep, we might as well do this right."

"I wouldn't say 'right,'" Grandpa teased, releasing me and turning his nose up at the packets of Swiss Miss. "But I'm fresh out of demerara sugar and dark chocolate. That will do in a pinch."

Grandma shushed him and told him to grab the marshmallows from the cupboard above the stove. We broke into the lemon crumb muffins as soon as the oven timer went off. And, with hot cocoa on the side, we filled our hollow bellies with sugar and one another's company.

When someone tapped at the window, the three of us jolted in our seats. Mr. Emerson was peering in. Grandpa motioned to the front door and opened it for him.

Aiden's grandfather had changed into dry clothes—gray and drab as usual. Something was different about him, though. I couldn't quite put my finger on it. The silence was uncomfortable as he shifted from one foot to the other and cleared his throat. "Sorry to disturb you. I noticed the light on and thought I'd check to see if there was any news on the little one."

Grandma's face was drawn. She patted her hair and cinched her robe tighter. She wasn't one for unexpected company. But she said, "Nonsense. You're always welcome here. If it weren't for you . . ." Grandma trailed off. "Well, you have our unending gratitude."

Grandpa placed a cup of steaming hot cocoa in Mr. Emerson's hands and smiled at him warmly.

"Lanie's mother called an hour ago," Grandma went on. "They're running tests at the hospital and keeping her for observation. They expect her to be fine—thanks to you and Liv."

Mr. Emerson's face broke into something not quite a smile, but close. He nodded his head and handed the mug back to Grandpa. "I can't stay," he said, offering no explanation. "As I said, just popped in to check on the girl." He tipped his head at my grandmother, then me, and started out the way he'd come in.

I don't know what got into me, but I sprang from my chair and followed him into the hallway. "Mr. Emerson, wait!" I hollered after him. When he stopped walking, I asked, "Why'd you do it?"

He gazed at me with a look so injured I had to take a step back. "You think I'd let a child drown?" he said, aghast.

"No. I mean . . ." I swallowed a lump the size of a sea snail. I didn't know how to express what I wanted to say. "Thank you. Thank you for helping Lanie. Thank you for everything. But I don't understand why you went into the ocean. Why did you save the turtle? All this time, I didn't think you cared what happened to them."

Mr. Emerson exhaled heavily and stared at something on the ceiling. It occurred to me what was different about him—the way he held his shoulders. He was a boxy sort of man—all rigid, hard angles. But now there was a curl to him that hadn't been there before—a softness.

"It's not that I didn't care." His chest heaved, then deflated. "Sometimes, adults confuse things—make them more complex than they need to be. Thanks for setting me straight."

A thought popped into my head. "Can I ask you something?" I said.

"I think you already did."

"Why did you turn all the lights off on Tuesdays?" I persisted.

Mr. Emerson's brow crinkled. "I'm afraid I don't know what you're talking about. Tuesday is my night off." He started to leave again, then tilted his head and added, "First thing tomorrow, come what may, I'll start calling contractors to make the inn more turtle friendly. Even if I get fired, it will be worth it to see Mr. Shaw's face when the bills come due."

Maybe it was a hot cocoa sugar rush, or I was still purging emotions, but I nearly bowled him over with a hug. He went still as a lamppost as I wrapped my arms around him. "Thank you!" I said again, squeezing him tightly. "Thank you, thank you, thank you!"

I pulled back and he was smiling. It was a small, delicate thing, like the gentle curve of a fragile shell. But, no doubt about it, it was a smile. It might've been the first time I'd seen his face truly brighten all summer. I decided right then and there that a hard-earned smile was the very best kind.

22

The average life span for a loggerhead sea turtle
in the wild is fifty or more years.

My grandparents and I eventually fell asleep on the
living room couches.

When daylight crept in through the windows the
following morning, we loaded up in the car, yawning, with
what was left of the lemon crumb muffins.

Lanie looked so tiny in the hospital bed, like a pearl nestled
in a clamshell. She was asleep when we arrived. Tubes ran like
tentacles from her arms, one hooked to a mask strapped to her
face. Machines whirred and clicked behind her. Mom rose
from a cot to greet us, stretching and feigning a smile.

Careful not to wake Lanie, I tucked her stuffed sloth next
to her on the bed.

"Water got into her lungs," Mom said shakily. "It caused

some inflammation and she's having trouble getting enough oxygen. They X-rayed her chest a little while ago . . . We're waiting for the results." Grandpa and Grandma surrounded her, and Mom fell into their embrace.

It occurred to me that I was adrift, standing alone outside their circle. That wasn't what I wanted anymore. I took a step forward, and Mom extended an arm and brought me in close.

When we broke apart, Mom half laughed, half moaned, "I desperately need some coffee." She swiped a tear with her thumb before it ran down her cheek.

"I noticed a café on the way in. She won't miss us if we're gone for a few minutes," Grandma said. Her lips pensively bunched together as she softly patted the base of Lanie's bed.

As they started to leave, I hung back. "Okay if I stay with Lanie?" I asked.

Mom glanced from Lanie's serene, waxen face to mine and nodded. She looked me deep in the eye and said, "I'd appreciate it if you did, Liv. Thank you."

She didn't veil her concern as she left the room a step behind Grandma and Grandpa. And the way she'd spoken—unsteady, but in a voice that was true and open—made me feel better and worse all at once. This was the Mom I'd been craving—not the one who'd been speaking in careful and unnatural tones any time things got uncomfortable. She'd been trying to hide her brokenness from me, like when she cried in the pantry. But it made me sad to think it took something like this, like my sister almost drowning, for her to let me see her real emotions.

But hadn't I been doing the exact same thing? Pretending everything was fine, trying to convince Dad and my friends I was having a good time so no one would worry about me? And then, when things got worse, instead of speaking up, I'd pulled away. That hadn't worked, either—Lanie lying before me in a hospital bed was the most unsettling proof it hadn't.

Yet she was still here because I *had* been there for her when she needed me. I didn't need to be perfect—things didn't need to be perfect—for me to be there for my family. Being myself was enough. And that's all I wanted from them in return.

Maybe that was part of growing up—realizing that life was full of contradictions. Like how you could feel the most alone in a crowd of people. And how you could be halfway across the country and still hold someone near in your heart. How people could have entirely different interests and personalities and still be close. How the person who annoyed you more than anyone else in the world could also be one of the people you cared the most about. I was pondering that particular contradiction when Lanie opened her eyes.

She sleepily pulled the mask away from her nose and mouth

and said my name. "Olivia." The wheeze in her voice was frightening.

"Shhh, don't talk," I said. "Put the mask back on."

She shook her head. "Did you find it?"

"Find what? The balloon? The turtle? Yes, we cut her free," I said, then inwardly scolded myself. Asking questions would only keep her talking.

"No, the mermaid tear."

"What?"

A nurse entered the room then and bustled up to Lanie's bed. "Oh no, not yet. You need to keep that on a little longer. Doctor's orders."

Lanie dolefully returned the mask to her face.

"It's supplemental oxygen," the nurse explained. "Her chest X-ray looked good. She'll need medicine to keep her lungs and blood healthy, but she'll be all right. Don't you worry."

The nurse patted my hand, and I realized I'd been holding my breath. He had crinkly lines around his eyes and mouth, and short, curly black hair. His smile was kind and reassuring. "I bet people tell you how much the two of you look alike all the time. I knew the moment I saw you that you were sisters."

I almost said, *No, people say I look like my dad*, but when I skimmed my sister's features, I decided that maybe some of me was mirrored in her, and vice versa. I shrugged and said, "I guess so." I was more like her, and she like me, than I'd ever wanted to admit.

Then the MOB arrived. We heard them coming long before they made it in the door of the hospital room. The twins entered first, darting right up to Lanie's bed. They shoved flowers in her face. Aunt Michelle and Uncle Angelo followed on their heels. Behind them, my mom and grandparents shuffled back in.

Lanie's eyes tracked the movement, and her eyebrows rose joyfully at the commotion. She was enjoying the attention.

Mom, on the other hand, tensed when Aunt Michelle glanced her way. I could tell she was expecting an "I told you so" from her older sister. Aunt Michelle had accused her of not keeping a close enough eye on us, and now here was Lanie lying in a hospital bed, having nearly drowned.

But instead of chastising her, Aunt Michelle reached out and pulled my mom to her. She clasped her hands. As she did, Mom's cell phone rang.

Mom broke away. "Sorry, I have to take this," she said. From the look on her face and the strain in her voice, I could tell it was Dad on the other end.

"Yes. She'll be okay," Mom spoke into her phone. "No, I don't know what her blood pressure is. Yes, I can ask . . ."

"Isn't there a rule about cell phones in hospital rooms?"

Aunt Michelle said snidely. She whipped toward Grandma while Mom continued to give Dad an update. "Can you believe him?" the MOB sneered. "Watch him grill her for a full medical report. I wouldn't be surprised if he tells the doctors what they're doing wrong. That man is ridiculous. An insufferable know-it-all."

Her words stung, but I didn't flinch. "That man is Lanie's and my father," I said, cool and calm. I wasn't hiding my emotions, but I was in control of them. "And he's worried." I didn't erupt the way I had when things upset me before, and I didn't bite my tongue, either. My steadiness surprised me, but something about what I'd been through in the past twenty-four hours made me feel I was capable of anything. I'd rescued hatchlings. I'd rescued my sister. I'd finally convinced Mr. Emerson to do something about the light coming from the Beachcomber. Me. Not Dad, not Aiden, not anyone else. I was a force to be reckoned with, and Aunt Michelle had pushed me too far.

"Of course Dad wants information," I continued. "How would you feel if you were thousands of miles away and found out Cisco or Diego nearly died? Wouldn't you want to know as much as possible about your kid's condition?"

Aunt Michelle measured me with her eyes. "Well, I didn't mean anything by it," she snapped.

"Yes, you did. You don't like my father and you never have, but that doesn't mean you get to say cruel things about him. You also don't get to decide where we live or tell my mom what to do."

Mom's eyes grew wide. She was still on the phone with Dad, but she'd overheard everything that had been said. Her lips curled into a smile, and she beamed at me with pride.

My aunt seemed as shocked as I was by my fledgling confidence. She gaped, but for once, she was at a loss for words.

The nurse stepped forward and politely suggested, "It might be best for Lanie if you take turns visiting. All this excitement isn't good for her."

Aunt Michelle looked at me, looked at the nurse, and nodded her head. She relented.

Grandma and Grandpa took the first shift. That way Mom could go back to the house to grab a hot shower, and the MOB could get settled in. On the way out of the hospital, Mom reported that Dad had booked a flight for the following weekend—as soon as he could possibly get away.

No doubt, the news made me happy. It had been a long summer without him. But it wasn't like on my birthday when I was so desperate to see him, I could barely stand it. I was excited he was coming, but I knew I'd be okay even if he didn't.

When we were back at the house, I snuck away to the beach as soon as I could. Aunt Michelle caught my eye as I was slipping out the back door. Her lips parted as if she had something to say about it. Then she clamped them shut, obviously changing her mind.

I ignored the daytime crowd and went straight to the dunes. Precisely where I'd seen Lanie before she'd galloped into the waves, I dropped to my knees and retrieved a single piece of sea glass. Drawing my legs beneath me, I sat in the hot sand and examined the mermaid tear. It was pure white, frosted like the rest, and yet it glistened like a diamond in the sunlight.

The beach, the people, everything faded away as I stared into the depths of the glass. It had been Lanie all along. She'd been the one planting mermaid tears for me to find. The realization caused a sudden ache in my chest. My six-year-old pinball of a sister had been coming here and secreting glass tears for me all summer. Even after I'd crushed her dreams and pushed her away, she'd braved the dark, and an imaginary monster, to leave me something she knew I'd treasure.

Lanie's determination surprised me. Her thoughtfulness touched my heart. It also didn't escape me that she wouldn't have seen the turtle if she hadn't gone out to the beach to leave this last mermaid tear. She never would've gone into the ocean and nearly drowned if I'd only gone with her.

The sea turtles, the mermaid tears, the lettered olive even—I'd resented Lanie for having one when I didn't—they were things I'd selfishly been pretending were mine and mine alone. They were things that made me feel connected to Dad. But Lanie had her own connections. She loved those things, too. I'd refused to see it because I didn't want to. I wanted memories of Dad, and treasured beach shells, and wildlife, and sea glass all to myself. Yet this whole time, she'd been reaching out to me, trying to be a part of my world again.

I felt like the previous night's storm had relocated inside me. My stomach roiled like the ocean waves. Just as when I'd been caught in the riptide, a feeling of helplessness returned. It was the same feeling as when I'd watched the turtle crawl ashore only to become distressed and turn away—the feeling that I couldn't fix anything.

But that was a lie—one I was sick of telling myself. I was strong. I had pulled Lanie from the violent waves. The same steadfast calm washed over me as when I'd stood up to Aunt Michelle. I wasn't perfect, but I wasn't powerless, either. I wasn't powerless at all.

Then it all came together. The pile of sea glass inside my drawer had grown to a mound over the summer. I had an idea for what to do with it, something I thought Lanie would like, and something that would help the turtles, too. I turned the sea glass around and around in my fingers, studying the way it shimmered like a gem. It just might work, but I would need Mom's help.

23

Loggerhead sea turtles have remained on the threatened species list since 1978. However, thanks to conservation efforts, population numbers are slowly starting to rise.

When we brought Lanie home two days later, I had everything ready—my heap of sea glass, plus a few things Mom helped me pick out at a craft store near the hospital: tiny sea turtle charms, fine silver chains, driftwood, and plastic lacing. Lanie grinned from ear to ear when she saw the items divided into neat piles on the dining room table.

Cisco and Diego played chase around the room. They swiped pieces of driftwood and used them as swords. I'd enlisted Grandma, Aunt Michelle, and Uncle Angelo's help getting things ready, and Mom, Lanie, and I took the open seats at the table.

My sister clapped her hands together excitedly. "It's perfect," she said.

During my visit to the hospital the day before, I'd asked her about the mermaid tears.

"How did you get so many?"

"Promise you won't be mad?

"Of course, silly," I said.

"Well, I found some on the beach, but then I couldn't find any more. So I asked Dad to send yours. Dad mailed them. Mom helped me stash them. Then each time you picked one up, I'd leave another one for you."

My mouth dropped open. "Mom and Dad were in on it, too?"

"You said you wouldn't get angry," Lanie reminded me.

"I'm not. I just . . ." I wasn't sure how I felt—like an outsider again.

"You were acting weird. Like a turtle, remember? We thought the mermaid tears might help."

Something shifted in my brain, and I saw it in an entirely different way. The whole time I thought I was adrift, my family had been casting a net around me, keeping me from truly slipping away.

And here they were now, most of them anyway, chipping in to help with something important to me. Lanie plucked a green mermaid tear from the pile of sea glass. Mom had used a Dremel tool to drill a hole in each one. I scooted my chair closer to hers and showed her how to make the necklaces Mom helped me design. We hung a single piece of glass and a small sea turtle charm on each silver chain.

"This one's yours," I said as I strung the prettiest one around her neck. Lanie held it away from her to inspect the turtle charm and sighed dreamily. I didn't have to ask if she liked it.

"Oh! And this is for you, too." I pulled a lettered olive out of my pocket. It had taken me hours to find it. It was smaller than the shell that had broken, but shinier. "Are you going to make a wish?" I asked.

She clutched it tight and shook her head. "Maybe later."

While I was presenting Lanie with her gifts, Grandma, Uncle Angelo, and Aunt Michelle threaded mermaid tears with plastic lacing and tied the strands to pieces of driftwood. The final product: wind chimes to tinkle in the breeze and reflect the sunlight. Again, my plan, Mom's creativity. Turns out, we make a pretty great team. The creations were even better than I'd imagined, and Mom shone with pride as her vision took shape.

"These are beautiful, sis," Aunt Michelle said.

"*Que lindo,*" Uncle Angelo added. "So pretty!"

Mom had always shied away from compliments, but she took these with her head held high.

Uncle Angelo went on to tell us about Glass Beach in Guantanamo Bay. "I used to walk it as a boy growing up in Cuba. The beach is littered with sea glass," he said. "Some of it is said to have washed ashore from rum bottles tossed into the sea by pirates long ago."

Diego shouted, "Argh!" and Cisco pretended to have a peg leg. They clanked their driftwood together.

"Each tumbled piece has had its own journey, its own story—like us, I guess," Angelo said, stringing several more together on a strand.

"Dad told me about that beach," I said brightly. "Here's a Forrester Family Fabulous Fact for all of you: Glass Beach collected so many mermaid tears because it has an odd shape. It's set back a little from the rest of the shoreline. With all the sparkling gems, it's called Pearl of the Antilles."

The mention of Dad just popped out of my mouth and no one even reacted. No one winced or squirmed in their seats. Aunt Michelle didn't sling any insults and even Mom smiled and said, "Pearl of the Antilles. I'd like to see that someday."

Phase two of my plan involved contacting the organization Sarah had given me the number for—the island turtle watch. The woman I spoke with confirmed that they relied entirely on volunteers. She said anyone could adopt turtle nests and make donations that went toward nesting supplies and educational materials and that funded the transportation of sick or injured turtles. I think I surprised her with my last question—one about the turtle watch and Tuesday nights, but when I told her why, she promised to meet me in front of the Beachcomber the following day.

After I got off the phone, everyone agreed selling the sea glass wind chimes and necklaces and donating the proceeds to the turtle watch was the best way to go. I snapped photos of our creations with my phone, then sent the pics to Dad and my friends. My phone hadn't stopped dinging since Mom returned it, and I'd finally responded to everyone back home.

Mia, Abigail, and Emily all wanted necklaces and Dad said he'd take two wind chimes for his apartment balcony. My heart ballooned. We weren't even finished making all the goods, and already we had five sales. It wasn't a bounty of riches, but it was something—enough to adopt a turtle nest.

Mom wondered aloud about opening an Etsy shop when we got back to Colorado. "I can sell the necklaces and wind chimes along with some of my paintings. What do you think?"

When we all said we loved the idea, and Lanie started making a list of the many things she could sell in her store, Mom's face lit as bright as the moon on a dark, clear night. She said we could order more sea glass online. Who knew how many more nests we could adopt by next summer?

The following morning, Aiden appeared at the front door with a goofy grin as wide as the sea. "Did you do this?" he asked. He grabbed my arm and pulled me onto the front step beside him.

I nodded and smiled as his grip slid from my arm to my hand. Fingers intertwined, we hurried next door. "My mom helped me make a few phone calls. Turns out the media thought an old man rescuing a child would make a terrific 'human interest story,'" I said.

"But you saved Lanie, too."

I shrugged. "I don't mind giving your grandpa all the credit, and Mr. Shaw was chomping at the bit for the positive exposure."

"I bet he was," Aiden scoffed.

News vehicles were scattered around the Beachcomber, and Mr. Emerson was being interviewed in front of the inn. Mr. Shaw stood beside him in a suit that was all wrong for the sweltering Florida heat. He dabbed at his forehead with a silk handkerchief.

"Ha, he looks miserable," Aiden noted.

"Just wait." I grinned.

We nudged in close to the swarm of newscasters and guests who had gathered on the front lawn. Mr. Shaw seemed totally unaware that the flower beds were being flattened beneath a mishmash of dress shoes, flip-flops, and loafers. He was beaming as one of the reporters asked Mr. Emerson about "saving a girl and a turtle all in one night."

Even though the question was directed at Aiden's grandfather, Mr. Shaw hogged the microphone. He spoke in a smooth and silky voice, proclaiming Aiden's grandfather a "highly regarded employee" and "local hero."

"Highly regarded employees and local heroes don't get fired," I whispered in Aiden's ear, and his eyes shimmered with delight behind his glasses.

I wanted to celebrate with him, but I couldn't yet. What came next would be harder. But if I'd learned anything the past few months, it was that sometimes things have to be said. It's not okay to pretend everything is all right when it isn't. And I couldn't wait around for someone else to act. Sometimes, it had to be me.

I let go of Aiden's hand and took a step forward. "Excuse me," I said, my voice ringing out above the others. I hardly recognized it as my own. My heart hammered in my ears, but I forced myself to keep talking. "Excuse me, Mr. Shaw?" I waited until I had everyone's full attention. The reporters, no doubt, were surprised to see me taking command of the press conference. They paused to listen to what I had to say.

"Why has the Beachcomber been turning off all the

outdoor lights on Tuesdays?" I knew the answer and would be more than happy to share it with the reporters, but first I wanted to see Mr. Shaw squirm.

He didn't disappoint. The owner of the Beachcomber glanced about at all the eyes bouncing from his face to mine. The crowd was expecting an answer. He tugged at his neck collar and smiled. "I'm sure I don't know what you mean," he said, trying to brush me off as quickly as possible. "Next question. Please."

"I'm sure you do," I shot back, fire igniting in my veins. But I took a deep breath and held my composure. "A volunteer from the island turtle watch walks your beach once a week to make sure there aren't any artificial-lighting violations. Somehow you figured out when they come by. You've been making the Beachcomber go dark on Tuesdays to make it seem like the inn isn't doing any harm. But it is. You are. You're endangering the lives of sea turtles."

"That's absurd," Mr. Shaw said, and chuckled lightly. At the same time, a thin stream of sweat trickled down his forehead. "We're not going to entertain the fantasies of a child, are we?" he petitioned the reporters.

Their silence and stern expressions said they were. One of the reporters, a man with a ski-slope nose, broad cheeks, and thick brown hair eyed me questioningly. When I nodded my approval, he pounced. "Mr. Shaw, are you aware it's illegal to interfere with the code enforcement of outdoor lighting of nesting beaches?"

"What?" Mr. Shaw, obviously rattled by the sudden turn the interview was taking, said, "I, um . . . yes . . . I mean, no."

"Mr. Shaw!" another reporter called out. "Why aren't the lights on the Beachcomber shielded?"

As the wolves circled, and Mr. Shaw flubbed all the questions thrown at him, a woman separated herself from the crowd and made her way toward Aiden and me. She was older than my mom but younger than my grandparents. She was wearing a bright-green SEA TURTLE WATCH T-shirt.

"You must be Olivia Forrester," the woman said as she sidled up to Aiden and me.

"That's right," I replied. "And this is my friend Aiden."

"I'm Rachel. Nice to meet you both." Her face was flushed with excitement. "I spoke with you on the phone yesterday, Olivia." She shook my hand, then Aiden's. "Thank you so much for reporting the Beachcomber's violations. I'll follow up with the appropriate authorities today—which should be fun after this conference." She grinned.

"Yeah," I said, imagining there would be no question of Mr. Shaw's guilt when the authorities watched the interview. But Mr. Shaw had a video as well . . .

"Rachel, I have to tell you something," I said, then proceeded to recount how I'd smashed the Beachcomber's light and how the whole thing had been caught on the security camera.

"Don't worry," she said. "After everything that's—"

"Come to light!" Aiden interjected brightly.

I teasingly rolled my eyes at him.

"Er, yes," Rachel continued. "I'm sure nobody will take any charges made against you too seriously. In fact, I'll mention that you're already doing community service by raising funds for the island turtle watch. On the other hand, I guarantee Mr. Shaw will be very sorry for his actions. Not to mention, this beach will be safer for nesting turtles from here on out."

I let out a heavy sigh of relief.

Rachel smiled. "Olivia."

"Yes?"

"Way to make a difference," she said, and shot me a thumbs-up. Even though it was corny, and Aiden was standing right beside me, I shot her one back. If he thought it dorky, well, so what.

After she'd walked away, I grabbed him by the shoulders. "There's no way Mr. Shaw can let your grandpa go now. And he has to fix the lighting!"

Aiden shrugged bashfully. Even though he was inches

taller than me, older and slightly more serious than he'd been in previous years, he seemed younger as he shifted beneath my embrace. "Thanks. I . . . I don't know what to say."

I wrapped my arms fully around him and pulled him close. "You don't have to say anything," I said. I heard a small gulp. Then, softly, he hugged me back.

"You know what this means, don't you?" I asked as we drew apart.

"What?"

"This isn't our last summer together."

Aiden's smile stretched impossibly wider across his face. I felt mine doing the same.

Aiden took my hand in his again. As we began walking back toward my grandparents' beach house, I was struck by how light and cheerful I felt. Despite all the sadness and uncertainty of the last few months, and the rocky times that were sure to come—they always did—in that moment, I felt nothing but joy.

. . .

The night before Dad was scheduled to arrive, Mom gave Lanie and me permission to go hunting for ghost crabs. We used red LED flashlights that wouldn't disturb the turtles. I leaned in close to my sister and whispered, "The turtles aren't bothered by the red light, but a squidopus *definitely* would be." Lanie giggled and raced ahead of me down the beach.

A wave of déjà vu washed over me as I watched her go. It was like our second night here, when Lanie followed me out to the beach. But it was way different, too. Things had changed so much. *We* had changed so much. Not just Lanie and me, but Mom also. We were all making an effort to be honest with one another. To be ourselves—not covering up our pain, and fear, and uglier emotions—but being kind to one another, too.

Earlier that day, I'd told Mom what I'd wanted to say ever since she and Dad announced the divorce. That I hated it. That it felt like they were killing something wonderful, and that I didn't understand why they had to split.

Mom didn't have answers for me, really, but she didn't give a canned response, either. We cried together, and that was enough.

"Lanie, wait up!" I called. I was out of breath when I caught up to my sister. "Let's go back to the dunes and rest awhile," I said.

We sat in the exact spot where she'd planted all the mermaid tears. It reminded me of the letter she'd slipped under the door the night she'd nearly drowned. The letter had crossed my mind several times since, but the moment hadn't been right to ask her about it until now. "You scratched out broken on your list," I said. "Then you wrote that our family is sea glass."

In the moonlight, I could see her head nodding. The unnatural triangle of light the Beachcomber had cast on the water was long gone. Mr. Emerson had hung some of our wind chimes near the pool. They tinkled in the wind blowing across the ocean. It sounded magical.

"Why?" I asked. I'd given it a lot of thought and was pretty sure I knew what she meant. But I wanted to hear it from her.

"You said our family is broken." I heard my sister drag in air, then exhale heavily, and I shifted my gaze to see her staring at the ocean. "Maybe you're right," she went on, "but bottles get broken, too, and the glass gets tumbled by the waves and turned into mermaid tears."

"Yes," I agreed.

"And mermaid tears are beautiful."

"Yes."

"So something wonderful can come from something broken," Lanie said. "Like sea glass . . . Like us." She reached for my hand. Months ago, I would have wriggled away, but now I grasped her fingers in my own.

She amazed me—my bold, creative little sister, who'd been battered by the ocean and came out stronger. We both had.

It occurred to me that magic does exist. Not in a spells and charms and fairy tales sort of way, but in the love we have for one another, and in the sometimes ordinary moments that change us forever.

I wasn't sure what life would be like back home as we adjusted to Mom and Dad being divorced. It would never be the same. But that was okay. Every heartache, every tumble, would only soften our sharp edges and make us more extraordinary. That is, if we allowed real magic to work its wonders.

I gave Lanie's hand a gentle squeeze. "I know exactly what you mean."

Acknowledgments

My gratitude for all who've helped with the creation of this book is as deep and as wide as the oceans.

My dear and brilliant editor, Mallory Kass, was beyond instrumental in transforming a budding idea about sea turtles into the story that appears on these pages. There are no words for how much I value her guidance, enthusiasm, friendship, and expertise.

I have endless appreciation for everyone at Scholastic. Special recognition goes to Jana Haussmann, David Levithan, and Maya Marlette.

I'm grateful for my lovely agent, Ginger Knowlton. It's an honor to be a Curtis Brown author.

Tara Dairman, Jessica Lawson, and Lauren Sabel deserve much credit for their timely and highly esteemed feedback on an early draft. And a shout-out goes to Marcel Fernandez for his eleventh-hour input.

My Colorado writing community is unparalleled. Sharing this journey with friends who also happen to write for kids has greatly enriched my life.

My friend Courtney Waters has kept me sane by lending a patient ear and sharing her wisdom over the years. Our conversations have influenced my writing more than she'll ever know.

James, Kristen, Madison, Macy, Lydia, and Noah Davenport didn't plan their trip to Anna Maria Island just for me, but it sure was convenient timing. Their "field research," photos, and stories spurred memories and provided a well of inspiration.

Ample recognition goes to my in-laws, the Goebels, for being all-around wonderful. I'll never tire of talking about books with Jane or exploring the ocean with Phil, Tim, and Kailey.

My parents, Lynn and Dale Davenport, gifted me with a childhood full of faith, love, and wonder, and have always encouraged my insatiable curiosity. My obsession with sea turtles began as a teen when my parents took me scuba diving in Akumal (which means *place of the turtles* in Mayan). They are ever my first readers. My gratitude springs eternal for their unwavering support and for blessings too numerous to count.

My husband, Matt, and our sons, Ethan, Logan, and Lucas, fill my days with more joy, adventure, and love than any one person deserves. They inspire me in big and little (squidopus) ways. My heart overflows with thankfulness that these are the people I get to share my life and dreams with.

Much love and appreciation to all the family and friends I cannot acknowledge here by name. Their encouragement means the world to me.

A thousand thanks to those working in any capacity to protect our oceans and marine life. They are my heroes.

Finally, above all else, the greatest glory goes to God.

About the Author

Jenny Goebel is the author of *Grave Images*, The 39 Clues: *Mission Hurricane*, and *Fortune Falls*. She lives in Denver with her husband and three sons. She can be found online at jennygoebel.com.